THE PERFIDIOUS CHIEF

James K Amoako

Dedication

You must love what you do, have a clear vision, and operate from a sense of purpose that is greater than yourself. Great leaders organize people around a shared vision.

I dedicate this book to my wife, Rose Tiokor Amoako, my children James Amoako Jr., Charles Appertey, Nicole Amoako, Jennifer Amoako, Viviana Amoako, and Audrey Samantha Amoako, as well as all my grandchildren and great-grandchildren.

They have all enhanced my life's journey, making it more meaningful!

Acknowledgements

Everybody at Adept Publishing deserves a great deal of thanks for providing me with the support, guidance, and professionalism that takes a mere idea and makes it into a book like the one you are reading now.

However, some people must be thanked individually for their special care, hard work, and contributions, as well as their unwavering support. Alexander Afriyie and Baaba Johnson enlightened me on cultural traditions.

I am particularly grateful to my brother Kwame Amoako's encouragement and support at every turn of this interesting journey. Kwame, thank you so much!

About the Author

James K. Amoako is a seasoned real estate professional and entrepreneur based in Laveen, Arizona. With decades of experience spanning real estate brokerage, appraisal, and finance, he brings a comprehensive understanding of the industry to every client interaction.

James holds an Arizona Real Estate Broker License and an Arizona Real Estate Appraisal License. He completed his Real Estate Broker Course at Westford College in Glendale, Arizona, and has continued his professional development through advanced appraisal coursework at the Arizona School of Real Estate & Business, covering residential report writing, site valuation, market analysis, and advanced residential applications. His academic credentials include a Master of Business Administration in Banking from Golden Gate University and a Bachelor's degree in Business Finance from California State University, Sacramento.

Since 2007, James has served as President and CEO of Abanex Realty in Phoenix, Arizona. As a designated broker and real estate agent, he specializes in representing financial institutions in real estate-owned transactions and serves as a Fannie Mae REO agent, guiding buyers and homeowners through short sales, federal and state incentive programs, and other real estate options.

Before founding Abanex Realty, James managed corporate operations at Appraisal Quest of Arizona, where he performed residential real estate appraisals and ensured compliance with industry standards. He began his career in the financial sector as a Financial Analyst and Accountant at Artec International, Inc., later joining the California State Banking Department, where he evaluated bank operations and regulatory compliance.

James is recognized for his ability to communicate complex real estate and financial concepts with clarity, providing clients with the guidance they need to navigate transactions confidently.

For inquiries, James can be reached at jkamoako@gmail.com.

Preface

This book, *The Perfidious Chief,* tells the story of a West African community fighting serious corruption. It is a powerful narrative about tradition, the strength of market women, and the sacred duties of chieftaincy. Beneath the story of rebellion and restoration, the events in Amansankrom offer a close examination of two key concepts in leadership: **Steward Leadership** and **Servant Leadership**.

This short introduction offers a way to think about these ideas before you begin the story. It will help you see Chief Kwaku Bonsam's harmful actions not just as personal greed, but as the failure of a fundamental social contract. The entire book can be understood as a case study, examining what happens when a leader fails and how a community must rebuild its ethical governance.

The Foundation of Leadership: Stewardship

In the traditional system that guides Amansankrom, the most essential duty of any leader is **Stewardship**.

This term positions the leader as a caretaker, not an owner. A caretaker is entrusted with essential things—resources, a mission, a vision, and people—by a higher power. They are charged to manage these things responsibly for the sake of the future. In Amansankrom, the Chief is the primary caretaker, or *Steward.* The higher power he serves includes the Ancestors from the past and the Future Generations. The Chief is, above all, a temporary manager.

The Stool's most important assets, which the Chief is sworn to protect, are:

- **The Land and Resources:** This includes cocoa farms, forests, and water resources. A good Steward protects these resources for the long term. The land is the town's lifeblood, and it must be conserved, not sold quickly for private benefit.

- **The Stool Itself:** This is the collective spirit of the people. The Chief must maintain its spiritual purity, follow all customs, and uphold the town's moral standing.

- **The Community's Mission:** The goal of the Chieftaincy is to ensure everyone in the community is well, resolve disagreements, and keep the people united. The Steward must always put the town's prosperity ahead of his own wealth.

The chief's downfall began the moment he refused to see himself as a mere guardian of the land. Kwaku Bonsam treated the entire kingdom and the sacred Stool as his personal property. He quickly moved to sell off the community farms. At the same time, he raided the treasury and pocketed large sums to enrich himself.

This is the failure of custodianship—and the start of all his trouble. The Queen Mother, Nana Adwoa, works to restore stewardship by creating the Communal Land Trust, making sure the land is forever safe from any single person's control.

The Daily Practice of Leadership: Servant Leadership

While Stewardship defines what a leader must protect and manage, **Servant Leadership** defines how the leader should act every day. If Stewardship is what the leader protects, Servant Leadership is how the leader interacts with the people.

A servant leader believes that their main purpose is to serve the followers. This idea shows up in key actions:

- **Empathy and Healing:** The servant leader strives to understand the people's concerns and actively works to resolve problems and bring people together.

- **Listenting and Awareness:** They consistently prioritize the needs of the community, particularly those of the most vulnerable voices, rather than issuing orders.

- **Commitment to Growth:** Everything they do is aimed at helping the community members become stronger, wiser, and more capable of leading themselves.

In a traditional place like Amansankrom, the chief is expected to listen to the Queen Mother and the elders, settle arguments fairly, and protect the vulnerable people—like the market women and the youth.

Kwaku Bonsam's second huge failure is giving up the servant role completely. He creates unfair taxes, ignores the voices of the market women who run the economy, and uses his power to hurt people, not help them. He acts like a master, not a servant.

On the other hand, the heroes of the book, Nana Adwoa and Akua Safoa, show true servant leadership. They spend the whole story listening to complaints, working to heal the town's broken trust, and guiding the people toward being strong on their own. Their focus is always on the welfare and growth of the community, even though it puts them at risk.

The crisis in Amansankrom comes from Kwaku Bonsam's failure on both counts: he failed as a Steward of resources and as a humble Servant to his people. He treated the town's wealth as his own and used his power to control and exploit the citizens. This broke the town's *Moral Economy*—the simple agreement that the leader would be fair and trustworthy.

The fight led by the women is much more than a political effort to remove one chief. It is a necessary movement to restore the ethical rules of governance. Their success is secured when they insist on clear **Financial Transparency** (making sure the Servant is always accountable) and strengthening the Queen Mother's Role (which acts as a permanent check on the Steward's power). The positive future for Amansankrom is not built on fighting, but on putting ethical stewardship and servant action into the town's new, lasting laws.

This book further confirms the lasting power of these ideas. It shows that, regardless of the culture or system, the moment a leader stops being a responsible caretaker and a humble servant, the throne, no matter how powerful, begins to lose its value.

The story of Amansankrom that follows illustrates these principles in vivid detail, showing how ordinary people—especially those whose voices are often ignored—can rise up to reclaim the moral authority of their town. It is a story of tradition, courage, and the difficult yet vital work of repairing what has been broken.

Prologue

Amansankrom nestles like a gem on Kwahu Mountain. Its terracotta-red tiled roofs shine bright in the sun, and its cocoa farms undulate down the hillside like a coverlet of fitted squares sewn by generations of gentle fingers. Early in the morning, when the mist wraps itself around the vales below, you can gaze out as far as the distant plains where the Volta River cuts its old path across the land.

This town—literally a "human settlement place"—has been here for three centuries. It existed before the British came and their maps and treaties, and before independence restored the Black Star to its rightful place. The Akan people, offspring of refugees from Kwahu wars, settled here among these hills. They came with their tongue, their ways, and most importantly, their political institution of chieftaincy—a sacred order designed to keep the people together, to adjudicate conflicts, and to hold the land in trust for generations yet unborn.

The town's landscape bears the marks of its history. At its heart stands the palace of Amansankrom, built of cement and stone, its courtyard shaded by a great odum tree that thrives through two rainy seasons. Surrounding it are the compounds of the royal family, then the elders' houses, and in widening circles, farmer dwellings, merchants, teachers, and artisans. Every fourth day, the market square bursts into life as women from nearby villages arrive to sell fruits and vegetables. Men gather in small groups, arguing over politics and football with the same restless passion.

Much of its past, Amansankrom flourished under wise stewardship. Chiefs came and went—some remembered as just, others as kind, a few for their errors. But they all had one plain credo: the stool—that venerated icon of power—wasn't theirs to claim. They were only its custodians, guardians of the people and the ancestors gazing from the beyond world.

The earth itself was a common trust. When the farmer required acres for his family to eat, the chief would give them to them. When the community required space for a clinic or school, the chief would give them that. This was the compact, unspoken but known by all—that the leader was filled with honor and respect, yet the nation was everyone's and no one's, a responsibility entrusted to the people generation to generation.

But human systems are vulnerable to human frailty. And a fault line develops in the ground—beyond sight initially, beyond awareness—until the entire web is liable to unravel.

This is the tale of such a fault line and the individual who blew it into a chasm.

This is the tale of Kwaku Bonsam and the gradual deterioration of Amansankrom.

Contents

Chapter 1: Daily Life in Amansankrom

In order to truly understand what Nana Kwaku Bonsam II took with him from Amansankrom, one must first understand what the town was like—not in some chivalrous sense of the past, but in the texture of daily life, in the rhythms that organized how people lived, worked, and dreamed.

Amansankrom existed in harmony with its fields, where every home stood close to the breath of growing crops. The villagers viewed the earth as both teacher and companion, shaping their days through patience, effort, and reward. Their prosperity reflected generations of intention and respect for the land. The red volcanic earth of the Kwahu Mountains was among the richest in all of Ghana.

Rainfall was regular; the climate was pleasant; and centuries of careful tillage had built soil that was almost alive with fertility. The town was rich because of the earth, and the richness of the earth had enabled Amansankrom to thrive in ways that most other rural towns could not. The major crop— the brown gold that connected Amansankrom to the global economy—was cocoa.

At harvest time, from October to December, the town came alive. Boys and men ascended into cocoa canopies, cutting off the football-shaped pods and lowering them in baskets. The pods were cracked open to spill out the prized beans inside, fermented in wooden tubs lined with banana leaves, and eventually dried on mats spread out across courtyards and rooftops. The smell during fermentation season was distinctive—a rich, earthy one that some found pleasant and others found barely tolerable.

Cocoa, though, would not have made Amansankrom successful. The land yielded cassava, plantains, yams, maize, and vegetables in remarkable variety as well. There were gardens of pepper that produced the fiery red and green chilies used in Ghanaian cuisine. There were pumpkin plots that fed families and provided seeds for next year's planting. There was ginger dried and ground to be used as medicine. There were pineapple fields on the slopes, and fruit orchards of mango, pawpaw, and guava trees so well tended that no living hand knew who had planted them.

This bountiful agriculture guaranteed food security was all but a certainty. Any household without land could feed itself for a year. There was always something to harvest, prepare, and save for better days. This security allowed people to pursue other endeavors—education, arts and crafts, public service, religious life—without the constant anxiety that afflicted communities where hunger loomed.

The Amansankrom farmers had learned how to farm with an intuitive instinct. They understood which crops did best in which soil, how to read the sky for rain or drought, and when to sow and when to harvest. Sons were taught by fathers, beginning when boys were small enough to ride on their fathers' shoulders as they strolled through the fields. It was not education in the classical tradition, but it was practical and inclusive. By his teens, any boy who paid attention could understand the subtle interrelation of human effort and natural processes that produced a crop.

Agriculture aside, hunting provided protein and companionship. During hunting season—roughly November to March—the men would set off into the mountain's slope forests in small groups for days. They hunted game birds, little antelopes, porcupines, and occasionally larger game like wild boars. The hunting was both functional and ceremonial. It was where young men staked out their courage and strength, where older men imparted knowledge of the forest, where stories were exchanged, and social bonds were sealed around fires at sundown.

But while agriculture was the domain of men, trade was the domain of women—and it was via trade that the true economic dynamism of Amansankrom was on display.

The women were the traders and entrepreneurs in the community. They were the ones who turned excess farm produce into commerce. Every market day—the fourth of the Akan cycle, occurring every nine days—the Amansankrom marketplace was bustling with women vendors. Hundreds of women laid out their goods in tidy heaps: pyramids of tomatoes, mountains of onions, baskets of oranges and limes, bundles of dried fish, packets of dried pepper, and containers of shea butter and palm oil, among many others.

These were no mere passive vendors waiting for customers to drop in. These women were shrewd businesswomen who understood profit margins, quality control, and customer relations with sophisticated instinctiveness. They knew their best suppliers, who the better payers were, what merchandise would be popular when, and why. They extended credit to loyal customers with frank discussions of payment. They negotiated hard but in good faith, realizing that today's demand for maximum profit would become tomorrow's loss of repeat sales.

Auntie Akosua was one of the best vendors in the neighborhood. In time, she would become a key figure in the community's refusal to back down to the chief. She had started decades earlier with a small vegetable stand and, through her intelligence, industry, and commercial skills, had built a network extending from Kumasi to other locations. She supplied individual vendors, restaurants, schools, and institutional cafeterias. Her success was not due to inheritance—she was born into a low-income family—but to her businesswoman's skills.

Women also operated the home economy. This was a more complex task than outsiders appreciated. It required a woman to stretch meager resources to feed her family, clothe her children, maintain the house, and fulfill communal responsibilities.

Auntie Akosua oversaw the storage of dry foods and the preservation of fruits and vegetables for times when the harvest ran low. Beyond that, she prepared cassava into fufu and gari, fermented corn for porridge, managed household resources like firewood and water, and carefully tracked community credit and debt.

Home management wasn't merely domestic duty—it was economic and social administration. A woman who couldn't efficiently manage her home might shame her family. A woman who managed her home successfully gained respect and authority that extended far beyond her own household. Mature women who had demonstrated good sense in managing homes came to be unofficial mentors to younger women, and their advice could shape community attitudes and policies.

Marriage in Amansankrom was nearly as much an economic partnership as it was a family tie. A man's prosperity was partially quantified in acres and farms, but the well-being and comfort of a family were just as much a result of the woman's ability to generate capital through bartering and processing farm products. It was not uncommon for the wife's earnings in trade to exceed her husband's earnings in agriculture—and this was accepted without ill will, as was possible in other societies.

The dynamics of marriage were marked by a shared sense of control, where each partner held influence in distinct areas of life. In matters of land and farming, the husband had precedence. In matters of home and domestic economics, the wife had precedence. A husband who tried too much interference with his wife's market enterprise was considered a fool. In the same way, a wife who tried to make unilateral decisions about agriculture without consulting her husband was considered disrespectful. The most successful marriages were those in which the couple knew and respected these distinct spheres.

Children were owned by their parents but raised in part by the community at large. It was presumed that any adult was qualified to discipline a disobedient child, that any household could feed a hungry child, and that the community was responsible for ensuring children received the education and moral uprightness needed to be good community members. That required more than one adult to monitor them and more than one source of advice and counsel. It also provided parents with assistance in raising children, so they were not left to do it alone, as would be the case in more isolated societies.

The pace of daily life in Amansankrom was governed by several calendars, one on top of another. There was a farming schedule that determined when the fields must be prepared, when seeds must be sown, and when harvests must occur. There was the market schedule—market day every ninth day, and women planned weeks in advance, cultivating or obtaining things to sell. There was the Islamic and Christian religious schedule, with observances and holidays that divided the year. Then, there was the traditional festival calendar of celebrations, remembering great moments in town history or transitions of the seasons.

In this rhythm of life, each day in Amansankrom unfolded with familiar predictability. The morning began before dawn, as women rose to begin household tasks—fetching water, kindling fires, and preparing food. By the time the sun appeared, the town was already alive with movement. Children made their way to school, farmers set out for the fields, and market women arranged their stalls for the day's trade. The noises of everyday commerce and conversation had awakened Amansankrom by mid-morning.

The warmth of midday signaled a break for lunch and rest. Whenever possible, families gathered for lunch, sharing both food and companionship. Afterward came a quieter stretch of light work—mending, visiting, or crafting—that bridged the afternoon hours. As the day wore on, energy returned to the fields, the markets, and the homes. When evening arrived, life softened into social ease: neighbors gathered to talk while finishing chores, children played in the dimming light, and men sat outside in small groups, exchanging stories, politics, and the day's news.

This daily life, this rhythm of labor and rest and sociability, had been refined over centuries. It worked. It served material requirements with room for social bonds, spiritual practice, and cultural transmission. It enabled people to manage themselves in work while connecting them to a broader society that provided security and meaning.

In this well-ordered world, Nana Kwaku Bonsam II introduced a new and corrosive influence: the commodification of everything and the aggregation of personal profit over collective benefit.

Under the previous chief, the relationship between the townspeople and their chief was customary but not forceful. The chief would attend local events, settle disputes, participate in celebrations, and determine how to parcel communal land according to need and custom. The people accorded respect to the chief, provided labor on communal ventures, and offered small payments on certain holidays. But these were regarded as reciprocal transactions—the chief giving leadership and defense; the people paying respect and labor.

Kwaku Bonsam revolutionized this relationship.

In his day, things were unstable and transactional. If you needed something—a favor, access to land, a feud settled in your favor, immunity from harassment—you had to give something back. It might be money, a percentage of business profit, loyalty, or popular support, regardless of what you thought yourself.

Auntie Akosua first made contact with this new world when she sought to broaden her trading relationships to include animals—goats and chickens for meat. She needed land to graze animals on and approached the chief with a proper request, as was the tradition.

"I would like to work on this area," she said. "It will provide employment for young men and provide a new source of protein for the community."

The chief listened graciously, then named a fee of fifty thousand cedis to occupy the land. This was not a charge for renting, which would have been fine. This was merely a bribe to the chief in order to allow her access to communal land.

Auntie Akosua was outraged. "Chief, the land belongs to the community. Traditionally, I only need permission from the council of elders."

The chief smiled thinly. "Times have changed, Auntie. The council of elders is advisory. I am the final authority on all land matters. If you wish to proceed, you will pay."

She paid, even if it took capital out of her trading operation and delayed expansion plans. But she paid because she understood what would befall her if she didn't: the chief could simply refuse her, or worse, use other means to hinder her business indirectly—delay in the processing of licenses, harassment of her suppliers, or sponsoring another trader who would compete against her.

The fishmonger Kwesi Mensah faced the same dilemma. He expanded his business to include dried fish in the Volta region, but fresh dried fish required a small refrigerated shop. Approval was required to build the shop, and so he visited the chief.

"I will give you the land," Kwaku Bonsam said. "But you must also arrange for my nephew to get work in your new shop and receive a share of the profits."

Kwesi had no choice. The chief's nephew worked for him, received a salary he barely deserved, and was awarded a cut of profits he had not earned. The arrangement was profitable for the nephew and acceptable to the chief, but it was corrupt and wasteful.

These individual transactions perhaps did not seem momentous in themselves. But collectively, they represented a radical shift in the chief's understanding of his office. He was no longer a trustee of the stool for the people. He was a trader employing power to enrich himself.

The women merchants spoke of this change incessantly in the market. They recognized it for what it was: a system of predation whereby the head used power not to promote the welfare of the community but to enrich himself. And they learned that their economic survival might hinge on their resisting as a group.

Early one morning, eighteen months into Kwaku Bonsam's reign, Auntie Akosua called an emergency session of the market women. More than fifty traders attended the meeting in the dark of the pre-dawn hours, before the market officially opened, and sat on benches and stools in the dusty marketplace.

"We're being squeezed," she told them baldly. "Every new business venture, every expansion, every upgrade—the head manages to squeeze payment out of it. We toil. We take risks. We build businesses. And then he takes a cut of what we've built—with no investment on his part."

"What can we do?" one of the younger traders asked. "He's got power. He's got the police. He's got power."

"We possess something more powerful," Auntie Akosua declared. "We possess the marketplace. We possess capital. We possess networks that extend throughout the region. We possess influence on what happens in this society because we provide the food, the commodities, and the commerce that keep Amansankrom operating. If we all resist together, he cannot disregard us."

She did not outline a particular plan that morning. But she sowed a seed. She made the women realize that they were not helpless—that their collective power could count.

The men were discussing similar topics in the villages and in the homes. The farmers were resentful of the chief's push for seizure of their fields. The hunters resented limits on hunting privileges. Young men who were expected to find work in community projects were shut out unless they paid or owed allegiance to the chief's group.

The daily life of Amansankrom continued on the surface. People still farmed, still traded, still raised families. But beneath the surface, a growing discontent spread like cracks in a foundation. And in that growing discontent lay the seeds of what would eventually become open conflict.

The Erosion of Trust

The impact of the chief's predatory system became most visible in the market square, where the pulse of community economic life could be felt directly. Merchants who had previously been successful started to struggle. Ama Boateng, a woman who provided cassava and cassava derivatives to markets around the area, discovered that after she paid the chief his "development fee" for increasing the size of her processing facility, she barely had enough capital remaining to buy supplies. Her margins, previously comfortable, became paper-thin.

"I am working from sunrise to midnight," she grumbled to Auntie Akosua on market day, her tone thick with weariness. "I get up before my household to begin the cassava processing. I don't rest until I have filled and marked everything ready for sale. And to what end? Half of what I now make goes to satiate the chief's appetite."

The worst was that the situation was arbitrary. There were no fees published and no open system of charges. The chief determined what one owed on the basis of his mood, his assessment of their capacity to pay, or his current need for money. One merchant could be charged fifty thousand cedis for a favor, and another could be charged double that for something exactly the same. This uncertainty bred resentment and anxiety much more profound than a definite tax would have caused.

Other traders attempted to avoid the system by keeping their businesses small and below the chief's notice. But this worked only so far. Mensah Rockson, the chief's pet councilor, had made himself into an unofficial monitor of market operations, and he would show up at the market requesting documentation for this sale or that one. If documentation was incomplete or lacking, fines were collected—and the fines necessarily ended up in the coffers of the chief.

Youths started to move away. That was perhaps the most revealing indicator of the town's change. Historically, young men from Amansankrom who traveled to the city for school or work would return with skills and capital to invest in their home village. They would settle on ancestral family farms, marry local brides, and raise their own children in the area where they were raised. This process had kept Amansankrom alive for centuries, giving it a steady flow of new ideas while preserving culture.

Under Kwaku Bonsam, all this changed. Young men who had finished school in Accra or Kumasi discovered very few prospects for them in their hometown. They could work on their families' farms if their families still owned land. They could work as hired hands on the chief's many projects. Or they could leave and never come back.

Kofi Osei, Kwame's younger brother, finished technical school in carpentry in Kumasi with distinctions and the promise of a successful vocation. Returning to Amansankrom with visions of opening a carpentry workshop—he had even been able to save enough capital to buy equipment and supplies—Kofi went to the chief for a piece of land in the center of town where he could open shop.

"I wish to have employment," Kofi told the chief. "I am able to teach young men about carpentry. I am able to make furniture and building supplies for the villagers and sell them to neighboring towns."

The chief listened, then named a steep price so high it plummeted Kofi's heart. It was well over five times the land's value and considerably more than Kofi had in savings. And, the chief continued, Kofi would have to hire the chief's cousin as a manager at a salary to be set by the chief.

Kofi was heartbroken after that meeting. Within two months, he sold his carpentry equipment and moved to Kumasi, where he later set up a thriving workshop in the city. He sent money back home to his aging mother on occasion, but he never returned to Amansankrom to reside. The village lost not only its labor and expertise but also the intangible value of having educated, ambitious young men who could be the future face of the town.

His tale was replicated again and again. Teachers who had finished schooling searched for jobs in major towns. Trained nurses from the capital found other places to work. Children of traders who had been promising pupils in school became professionals in urban areas. Slowly, Amansankrom lost some of its brightest and most ambitious young people.

It also had a substantial impact on community decision-making. Decisions regarding significant matters were traditionally made by councils comprising both experienced elders and younger men who brought in new ideas. Young people left behind skewed the power base toward the elderly, making it easier for the chief to keep things under control. The individuals who could have opposed him most successfully were absent.

The relationship between the chief and the farmers also broke down, although more gradually than with traders. Farmers were less attached to the soil than traders were to the marketplace. But even they came to resent the chief's control.

New "agricultural development fees" were imposed. Farmers who wished to utilize enhanced seeds paid the chief a percentage. Those wishing to form cooperatives paid the chief for his permission. When cocoa prices increased on the global market and farmers saw temporary prosperity, the chief created a special "town development levy" that took much of their windfall profits.

Joseph, Kwame Osei's father, had a small cocoa farm that was a three-generation family business. He was not rich by any means, but he was content. The farm yielded sufficient cocoa to sell for profit, sufficient food crops to sustain his family, and sufficient excess to assist relatives in crises. It was a simple but viable existence.

Joseph's condition had worsened significantly two years into the new chief's reign. He was paying fees for this and that, levies for one thing and another, and he discovered that his capacity for saving had plummeted. Where once he may have saved enough to invest in upgrading his farm—clearing more land, acquiring superior tools, upgrading his drying facility—he now struggled to keep what he had.

"The chief is quietly killing us," Joseph ventured one night as he sat with his son Kwame. "Not suddenly, not in a manner that brings instant crisis, but quietly, like a disease that consumes the body from the inside out. We have food to eat. We have a roof over our heads. But we have no future. We are unable to improve. We are unable to save. We can only survive."

The psychological effect was deep. Amansankrom was a society where individuals could reasonably anticipate bettering their lot through diligence and good husbandry. A farmer might dream of increasing his farm. A trader might dream of developing a bigger venture. A youth might dream of acquiring an education and coming back to give back to society. These aspirations had been the driving force behind community dynamism.

Under Kwaku Bonsam, those dreams perished in large numbers. Folks learned not to expect too much, not to invest too much, not to plan too far ahead. The future was no longer certain, and uncertainty led to a kind of spiritual burnout.

This fatigue could be seen in small things. The work done on collective projects suffered. When the chief said a trail had to be fixed, individuals did the bare minimum instead of taking pride in quality performance. When community service was called for, individuals showed up but without passion. The mutual relationship between the chief and the people had been destroyed and replaced by an extractive one, and individuals reacted by withdrawing emotional investment in collective well-being.

The market had always been a place of noise and warmth, a living pulse at the center of the town. Lately, that pulse had slowed. Trade continued; coins still changed hands—but the laughter that once joined strangers had grown scarce. The people still gathered, yet they no longer seemed together. More transactions were purely transactional—products traded for cash, nothing more. The social connections that had made the market a hub of community activity diminished.

But it was just this deterioration that the power of resistance among the community began to coalesce. The traders, and particularly the women traders led by Auntie Akosua, organized an informal network. They started to collude, inform one another of the chief's latest plots, and talk about how they would defend their businesses and livelihoods.

Through informal circles based on mosques and churches, the peasants started openly sharing their complaints. A peasant who had lost land due to the chief's machinations would relate his tale in a whisper after Friday prayers or after Sunday services, and the tale would spread, generating solidarity and awareness that the issue was structural, rather than personal.

In his classroom, Kwame Osei observed that his students were increasingly interested in studying justice, government, and history. When he lectured on the ancient Akan kingdoms and their checks and balances on chiefly power, the students leaned forward in rapt attention. When he spoke about how other societies had reacted to oppression, they asked thoughtful questions about whether rebellion was feasible and what ordinary folks could do to shape their leaders.

He started to see that his documentation work could be even more significant than he had originally thought. The youth of Amansankrom—those growing up under the rule of the new chief—had to be made aware that this was not the norm, that this was not how chieftaincy was meant to work. They had to be shown proof, in writing, that there had been another path—that their village once worked along different rules.

One night, Kwame decided. He summoned three of his closest students to his house, among them Abena's older cousin, a girl named Yaa who was particularly bright and inquisitive. He revealed to them his secret ledger for the very first time.

"See this," he said to them. "This is a record of what our chief has done to our people. Read it slowly. And consider what it signifies."

The children read quietly, their faces becoming more and more grave as they took in the proof of institutionalized corruption, intimidation, and exploitation. When they were done, they glanced at Kwame with a mixture of sadness and resolve.

"What do we do with this?" Yaa asked. "Can we let people know? Can we let them see what he's doing?"

"Not yet," Kwame replied cautiously. "First, we collect more evidence. We record everything. We ensure that when the time is right, when people are prepared to call for justice, we have evidence that cannot be ignored."

He wasn't sure if that day would ever arrive. But he realized that if it ever did, evidence would count. The chief could bully individuals. He could influence council votes. He could bribe individual officials. But he could not easily silence a written record made by a multitude of people, scattered in many places, impossible to eradicate in full.

The seeds of resistance that had been sown at Auntie Akosua's market meeting and watered in innumerable hushed conversations were starting to germinate. They would take decades to mature into something tangible enough to defy the chief's authority. But they were germinating—beneath the surface and out of sight—fueled by the daily reality of oppression and the basic human impulse for dignity and justice.

Amansankrom was a village in transition during these years, although the majority of people were not yet aware of the extent of change. On the surface, life went on. Cocoa was picked. Markets opened. Children were born and reared. But the social contract of the village had been cracked, and the tension gathering force beneath the surface would one day have to be released.

Chapter 2: The Rise of Kwaku Bonsam

The troubles started, as troubles do, with a funeral.

When Nana Ampadu Okyere III passed away during the harmattan winter of 2003, the whole town of Amansankrom was in mourning. He had reigned for thirty-two years, a reign recalled as a time of steady advancement. The town acquired electricity, a secondary school, and a health clinic during his reign. He resolved land disputes with Solomon's wisdom and Job's patience. When the government needed to put a new superhighway through the town's agricultural land, he had brokered compensation that worked for every family involved. In all measures, he was a chief in the best sense of the word.

His death created a void that nature—and human desire—detested.

By tradition, the new chief must be appointed by the queen mother in consultation with the council of elders, selected from among the qualified members of the royal family. The qualifications were obvious: the contestant must have sound character, high esteem in society, knowledge of tradition, and a desire to serve the people and not himself.

There were three clear contenders.

- The late chief's nephew, Kofi Mensah, was a retired headmaster who had a reputation for integrity and scholarship.

- Yaw Donkor, a prosperous businessman who had established a chain of pharmacies in Accra, had over and over again shown his devotion to Amansankrom by providing scholarships for the town's children.
- And then there was Kwabena Asante, a reserved lawyer who had devoted years to fighting land rights cases for rural communities.

Kwaku Bonsam was not among them.

He was, at best, a remote cousin of the royal lineage—so removed that his claim needed a genealogist's chart and a very liberal interpretation of family trees. He had departed from Amansankrom twenty years before as an unrespectable young man, who was said to have been mixed up in all sorts of minor deceptions. He came back for the funeral riding a Land Cruiser with dark glasses, sporting golden rings on both hands, and issuing promises that turned out to be too good to be true.

"I will bring progress!" he declared at the funeral ceremony, his thunderous voice echoing through the courtyard. "I have friends with the decision-makers in Accra and in the ministries. Amansankrom will have tarred roads, a new market, and a technical institute under my rule. I will make this town the glory of the Kwahu Mountain!"

The elders looked at each other doubtfully. The queen mother, Nana Akosua Serwaa, a seventy-year-old woman whose keen eyes saw all, sat in silence. But Kwaku Bonsam had not come back empty-handed or otherwise. In the succeeding weeks, while the town finished the funeral ceremonies and prepared for the selection process, things started to go wrong.

Kofi Mensah, the retired headmaster, unexpectedly declared he was pulling his name out of the running. People close to him were stunned—he had been eager to help the community. But that was all the reason he gave in a brief statement about "family considerations." It was rumored that his son, a contractor in Accra, had threatened to lose valuable government contracts.

Pharmacy owner Yaw Donkor had to contend with surprise tax issues. Executives from the Ghana Revenue Authority swooped down on his shops with charges of wrongdoing. The charges were later withdrawn, but not before exhausted and preoccupied Donkor indicated privately that he could no longer shoulder the duties of chieftaincy during such adversity.

Kwabena Asante, the attorney, was more tenacious. He publicly challenged Kwaku Bonsam's authenticity as a candidate for the throne and demanded an open selection process. Two weeks later, his home in Amansankrom was broken into—nothing valuable was stolen, but his personal documents were left scattered all over, and a message spray-painted on the wall of his bedroom: "Wise men know when to step aside."

The queen mother did not waver. She asserted that Kwaku Bonsam's title to the stool was weak at best and that the town was entitled to better leadership. But she was elderly, and her power, while revered, was not total.

Kwaku Bonsam drew on his last ace.

He took the whole council of elders to Accra, where he put them up in a top hotel. There were encounters with government ministers who sang Kwaku's praises. There were envelopes, handed over quietly, full of money more than what most of these men took home in a year. There were behind-the-back offers of chieftaincy titles for their own sons, of contracts for their companies, of issues that could be waved away and prospects that could become available.

By the time they made it back to Amansankrom, the tide had shifted.

Installation was performed on a Saturday in March 2004. Though the queen mother protested and many townsfolk were uneasy, Kwaku Bonsam was still enstooled as chief of Amansankrom, even as several elders refused to attend. He adopted the stool title Nana Kwaku Bonsam II—a move that caused surprise, since the original Kwaku Bonsam had been a nineteenth-century chief who was remembered more for his brutality than for his sagacity. Maybe the new chief wasn't aware of this history. Or maybe he just didn't care.

The ceremony was extravagant by Amansankrom standards. Three goats were sacrificed rather than the usual one. A well-known Kumasi highlife band was hired. Accra politicians showed up, their presence adding to the legitimacy of the event. Kwaku Bonsam sported kente cloth so complicated that it likely cost more than most Amansankrom families earned in six months.

In his inaugural speech, standing in the palace courtyard with his hand confidently on the holy stool, the new chief waxed lyrical about the future.

"My people," he announced, "the day has arrived when a new era has begun for Amansankrom. We lived well in the past but must open ourselves to the future. With me at the helm, this town will flourish as never before. We will get investors. We will farm our land. We will be wealthy!"

The people clapped, although some of the elders picked up on the fact that he used "we will get rich" instead of saying "we will all become wealthy." It was a subtle difference, easily missed in the heat of the moment.

But words betray truth, and eventually, that truth would be gruesomely apparent.

Among those standing at the periphery of the throng was Kwame Osei, a secondary school teacher and grandson of the late Nana Ampadu Okyere III. He did not clap. He stood, arms crossed, face somber, as next to him, his wife, Ama, grasped the hand of their infant daughter.

"This is not right," Kwame whispered to his wife. "My grandfather would be ashamed."

Ama pinched his arm. "Maybe he'll learn the job. Maybe the job will transform him."

But Kwame just shook his head. He had observed Kwaku Bonsam's eyes throughout the speech—eyes that hadn't looked out at the people in love or obligation, but in calculation, as if he was inspecting not a community but a resource to be used.

"No," Kwame said softly. "I don't think so."

He was indeed correct.

Nana Kwaku Bonsam II expressed his true character six months after consuming the stool. He first made known his intention that all decisions concerning land allocation would now be taken by him directly, without going through the council of elders, as was the custom. When the council protested, he waved his ringed hand away as if brushing aside an unwanted insect.

"Times have changed, old men," he said to them. "The chief must be able to make fast decisions if we are to grow this town."

The second indication was when portions of communal land—fertile agricultural land that several families had cultivated for generations—were unexpectedly deemed "available for development" and auctioned off to outsiders. The proceeds of these sales never materialized in any community ledger. When asked about them, the chief asserted that it was being kept "in trust" for upcoming projects that never quite happened.

The third indication was when individuals who criticized the chief too vocally started experiencing issues. Their small business loan applications were withheld mysteriously. Their cases in the chief's court were decided against them. Their kids were denied opportunities.

A culture of fear started settling over Amansankrom like nightfall mist.

And Kwame Osei, the instructor, started to take notes. He documented all the questionable choices, all the parcels of land, all the spoken rumors of intimidation. He had no idea what he would do with this data, but some instinct told him it would prove significant.

His grandfather had done the same during a hard time in the town's history. Kwame had discovered them after the old chief's death—meticulous records that had settled a large land contest years later.

Maybe, Kwame believed, history was on the verge of repeating itself. And maybe, this time around, the outcome would be different.

Consolidation of Power

Nana Kwaku Bonsam II's first year in office slipped by like a painful fever—irksome but not intolerable yet. The town grew accustomed to its new status the way the body grows accustomed to an incurable sickness, tolerating the discomfort because there appeared to be no quick solution.

The chief acted fast to consolidate his authority. He replaced some of his long-time council members with younger men—men who owed their membership to him outright and thus were likely to owe him loyalty, not wisdom. These new councilors were ambitious men on the periphery of community life who had always felt neglected and now enjoyed the new vitality they brought. They were the chief's ears and eyes around Amansankrom, coming back and telling him who had said what in the market square, which elders complained at community meetings, which families could be plotting to overthrow his rule.

Among these new councilors was Mensah Rockson, a man in his late thirties who had failed in various businesses and attributed his failures to other people instead of his poor decision-making. The chief promoted him to be the leader of the Land Management Committee—a new post that vested Rockson with the power to be in charge of all land transactions in Amansankrom. It was putting a famished dog in control of the butcher's shop.

"Development calls for courageous decisions," the chief declared after some elders challenged Rockson's selection. "Mensah is familiar with the new economy. He will assist us in getting the right investors."

What "the right investors" really meant was soon revealed. They were the chief's friends in Accra—middlemen and speculators who viewed Amansankrom's perch on the Kwahu Mountain as a perfect location for weekend retreats and vacation homes for rich city dwellers. Land that had been worked for generations to produce cocoa and cassava was now rezoned for housing development. Farmers who tilled these lands were presented with two options: take pennies as payoff or be evicted.

Kofi Darko, a farmer who grew cocoa and whose family had been working the same five acres for four generations, was one of the first to fight back. He was a stout fifty-year-old man with hands calloused by decades of rural labor and a reputation for speaking his mind.

"This soil provides for my family," he said to Mensah Rockson when the councilor arrived with documents for him to sign. "My grandfather cleared it by hand. My father planted the cocoa trees. I've enriched the soil and constructed the drainage. You can't simply take it."

Rockson smiled—a poor, thin smile that never quite extended to his eyes. "No one's stealing anything, brother Kofi. We're paying you a good price. Twenty thousand cedis. You'll make more money than that from cocoa in five years."

"And what will I do when those five years are up? Where will my children plant? Where will their children plant?" Kofi shook his head. "The answer is no."

The smile left Rockson's face. "You are making a mistake, my friend. The chief doesn't like individuals who get in the way of progress."

"Then the chief and I don't agree on what progress is."

Kofi Darko had returned three weeks earlier to find his cocoa trees dying. They had been poisoned overnight with a dose of herbicide pumped into the trunks. Years of tender cultivation were wiped out in a moment of sabotage. When he went to the police, they listened to him with evident unconcern and did nothing. When he attempted to bring his case before the chief's court, he was informed the chief was busy at present to hear cases concerning land.

In the end, with his livelihood lost and no access to legal remedy, Kofi settled for the lesser compensation of fifteen thousand cedis—scarcely sufficient to lease a small store in town and attempt to begin anew as a petty trader. He was fifty years old, and all he knew about life concerned farming.

At his cocoa trees' funeral—for that was what he referred to as the day he finally abandoned his land—he stood at the border of his poisoned grove, and tears were running down his weathered face.

"They have not only killed trees," he told the small group of neighbors who had come to console him. "They have killed our way of life. They have killed the covenant between chief and people."

His tale passed through Amansankrom like a cloud of smoke, with the pungent odor of warning. Other farmers, watching what became of Kofi Darko, sold their lands without a murmur. It was less difficult to yield than to resist.

Not everybody yielded quietly, however.

Teacher Kwame Osei watched these events unfold with growing apprehension. He kept detailed records that had become an elaborate log, noting every dubious land deal, each act of intimidation, and every moment when the chief's interests clashed with the community's welfare. He stored this log in a locked filing cabinet in his classroom, under a pile of dusty old math textbooks no one ever troubled to read.

His wife, Ama, was concerned about his fixation. "What good will these notes be?" she asked him one night as he sat at their tiny dining table, scribbling by the light of a lamp while their daughter Abena slept in the room next door. "The chief has the power. The elders are fearful. The police do nothing. Who will care about your records?"

Kwame set his pen down from his writing, his tired eyes set in determination. "I don't know yet. But my grandfather taught me that truth is powerful even when it appears so weak. He said that injustice multiplies in the dark, but documentation shatters the dark. Perhaps today no one will hear us. But one day, someone will. And on that day, they will have to have evidence, not just tales."

"And what if the chief finds out about what you're doing? What if Mensah Rockson or one of his spies discovers it? They might give us a hard time, Kwame. Consider Abena."

"I'm thinking about Abena," Kwame whispered. "What are we going to do, build an Amansankrom where she will come if we all keep quiet? What are we going to tell her when she asks us why we did not move when her grandfather's legacy was being pulled down?"

Ama sighed, knowing that it was futile to argue further. Her husband had not just inherited his grandfather's papers, but also his sense of responsibility. It was both his greatest strength and, she feared, his biggest weakness.

In the meantime, the chief became more audacious with each passing month. He ordered a new palace—not a restoration of the ancient building that had been the residence of chiefs for centuries, but a completely new one on the periphery of town. It was a gaudy three-story house with pillars striving to be as grand as the pillars of Greece but ending up as pretentious, neon yellow-painted, with a crimson roof visible from miles away.

"The old palace is not suitable for a modern chief," he replied to the question of cost. "We want to present visitors with the fact that Amansankrom is a modern town."

No one knew the mansion's cost because the chief had not given accounts. However, Accra contractors were paid in cash from sources that continued to remain mysterious. They attributed it to sales of the town's forest rights to a timber company, from clandestine transactions with mining explorers keen to exploit the mountain's mineral wealth, and from brokerage on each block of communal land sold to developers.

The queen mother, Nana Akosua Serwaa, went on complaining about the chief's extravagance. Even in her old age, she was intelligent and obstinate. She denounced the new palace as a waste of funds that could be channeled into the welfare of the people.

"A leader has to be among his people, not over them," she said in a public forum. "This mansion is no palace—it's a symbol of one man's ego."

The head smiled at his words, but his eyes were hard. "The queen mother is old," he told his advisors later. "Old people are stubborn. They hold on to things as they were because they have no future. We should be patient with her, but we cannot let her stand in the way of progress."

But to be "patient" with the queen mother was another matter. She was kept increasingly out of key conferences. Her opinions were ignored when decisions were made. Her traditional right to make land decisions was duly disregarded. When she complained, she was treated with ceremonial courtesy but practical exclusion—like a valued guest at a party who is no longer invited into the bedroom where serious matters are under discussion.

The chief's exclusion of the queen mother was likely his greatest mistake. She had been the conscience of Amansankrom for decades, and even those who opposed her did not necessarily do so in an insulting way. By leaving her out, the chief lost the support of many who had been willing to take him at face value.

Among them was Auntie Akosua, the richest market woman in town and a relative by marriage of the queen mother. She had a retinue of traders who supplied goods not just to Amansankrom but to several neighboring towns as well. When she spoke, everyone listened—not because she was a formal personage, but because she knew business and human nature as well as anyone else.

One night, Auntie Akosua had a group of powerful women over to her compound for a "small party." Twenty women attended—traders, teachers, nurses, and chiefs' wives. They sat in a circle in her courtyard, drinking sobolo and snacking on kelewele as the children played in the yard opposite.

"We need to discuss what is going on in our town," Auntie Akosua declared after the women had sat down. "We need to discuss this chief and what he is doing to us."

The women looked at each other. Everyone understood what she was saying, but to openly complain about the chief was dangerous.

"He has spies everywhere," one of the women said nervously. "Even here, who knows who reports to Mensah Rockson?"

Auntie Akosua's tone was firm. "Then I'll say it straight: I owe obedience to nobody but my conscience and forebears. The spies who came to observe us may leave now."

There was no movement.

"Good," Auntie Akosua went on. "Listen to me now. The men—the elders and councilors—have let us down. Some of them are corrupt, some of them are cowards, all of them are useless. If Amansankrom is to be saved, it will be saved by the women. We have always been the foundation of this society. It is time we remembered it."

This was the start of something new in Amansankrom—a stillness of resistance that would expand and one day be something the chief could not bully off or disregard. But that would have to wait.

For the moment, as the first year of the reign of Nana Kwaku Bonsam II drew to a close, the town accommodated itself uneasily to its new situation. The chief grew richer and more arrogant. His supporters grew rich at the expense of the resistors, who were bleeding. The palace and people grew further and further apart day after day.

And in a tiny high schoolroom, a teacher named Kwame Osei began filling his secret ledger with meticulous noting, building a ledger one day that would be more impactful than anyone had ever conceived.

Chapter 3: Traditions and Culture

If you asked the elders at Amansankrom to explain to you what made their town unique, they would not mention the rich soil or thriving cocoa plantations last. They would not mention the busy marketplace or successful merchants. They would mention something less tangible but more vital: customs that were handed down from father to son, cultural rituals that tied the people together as tightly as the threads in a good cloth.

Amansankrom was something more than a cluster of individuals who simply existed in close proximity. It was a living stockpile of culture, a nation united by habits of behavior that had been centuries in the making, habits that imparted life with something greater than mere efforts at achieving material existence. But it was a mixed cultural heritage—a patchwork woven from beautiful and ugly threads, a heritage of traditions which had pushed the village forward and traditions which had pulled it back, practices they had struggled to retain and practices they had struggled to eradicate.

The people of Amansankrom were Kwahu, members of the dominant Akan ethnic group that controlled most of southern Ghana. The Kwahu maintained their own unique identity within the Akan kinship—they were renowned across all of Ghana as traders and entrepreneurs, as individuals who blended enterprising talent with deference to tradition. "Kwahu nni dam" was a proverb throughout Ghana: "The Kwahu man does not get drunk." It did not mean that Kwahu men did not drink, but that they were never out of control even when enjoying themselves, that they never left their duties for anything.

It was not an abstracted cultural identity. It was everyday lived in modes of being, ceremonies, festivals, and the myriad tiny traditions that governed the way one treated other people and had a sense of where they were in the world. The Kwahu language—a local Twi language with its own distinct pronunciation and lexicon—was the medium through which this culture was passed down. Proverbs and sayings peppered everyday speech, each one imbued with the wisdom of generations.

"Se wo werɛ fi wo dee a, ɛnkyɛ biara na obi de ne dee bɛma wo," they'd say. "If you forget your own, it won't be long before someone gives you theirs." That is, if you forget your culture, someone else's will fill the void. And not always for your benefit.

The customary social organization in Amansankrom was premised on the extended family, or *abusua*. One belonged to his mother's line—the Akan being matrilineal—and through that line received not only property rights but also identity, duties, and religious affiliations. The household head, or *abusuapanyin*, adjudicated among household members, held and managed household property, and spoke for the household in situations involving the community.

Outside the family were the different clans, each with their own history, taboos, and totems. Asona clan, for example, claimed descent from the founders of most Akan states and adopted parrot as their totem. Members of the Asona clan were prohibited from killing or eating parrot. The Oyoko clan, which was royal in most Akan societies, adopted the falcon as their totem. These affiliations with clans built networks of reciprocal aid and indebtedness that stretched well beyond Amansankrom proper—a Kwahu visitor might be received by clan members in remote towns, building a personal network throughout the region.

There was religion in Amansankrom as well, which was diversified and stratified. The majority of families were Christian—Presbyterian, Methodist, or Pentecostal—having been converted during colonialism or in the very early post-independence years. There was a notable though smaller Muslim community, clustered in one quadrant of town, whose members had originally migrated from the northern territories centuries ago and who had been integrated into the society while retaining their religion.

But under these monotheistic faiths lay an earlier layer of belief that did not entirely pass on. The ancestors were still honored, still called upon, still thought to take care of the living. Libation was offered at significant events, invoking the ancestors to witness and bless the event. Sacred groves remained untouched by development, pieces of land inhabited by spirits and on which no man ever envisioned cultivating or constructing. The river that runs through the valley below Amansankrom was also said to have a spirit ruler, and it was sacrificed to when dry or in flood.

This syncretism of Christian or Islamic faith and pagan religion was not experienced as contradictory. The woman would attend Presbyterian church on Sunday, hold a libation ritual on Tuesday, and experience no contradiction in it. God was God, the ancestors were the ancestors, the spirits were the spirits. They were in other but the same universes, and a wise person remained on good terms with all of them.

The chief's function here was religious and political. He was neither administrator nor judge. He was the living connection between individuals and their ancestors, guardian of tradition, personification of past and present continuity. And therefore, the installation ritual was so complex, the chief was purified and transformed in ritual, he assumed a stool name linking him to previous chiefs.

The stool itself—tangible thing upon which the chief sat for ceremonies of great import—was not just furniture. It was said to be imbued with the people's soul, the collective knowledge and spiritual power of all past chiefs. To be disrespectful to the stool was to be disrespectful to the ancestors. To employ the stool's power for hidden agendas was to be a betrayer to what it stood for.

This was the deeper motivation behind Kwaku Bonsam's corruption. He was not just an evil politician or a crooked businessman. He was throwing away the sacred trust, employing religious power for evil ends, violating the covenant between the living and the dead, and the unborn. This automatically perceived the elders, though they could not always say it in exactly those words. Their resistance to his reign was more spiritual than political, stemming from a perception that something sacred was being violated.

Akwasidaekese: The Sacred Festival

Amansankrom's ritual calendar and festivals that divided the year were simultaneously a time of celebrating culture and re-establishing community ties. Of all the celebrations, however, none surpassed Akwasidaekese—the Great Sunday Festival—held on the Akan month of Opepon, or March or April in the Western calendar.

Akwasidaekese was not one day but a season, weeks during which the whole society united to honor the ancestors, the harvest, and their commitment to one another. It was the moment that migrant relatives who went away to settle in the towns came back home. It was the moment that all quarrels that existed throughout the year were legally settled. It was when the young people were initiated into manhood. It was when the chief confirmed his place as the religious and political hub of the community.

Arrangements for Akwasidaekese started weeks beforehand. The houses were cleaned and repaired. The roads were scrubbed. The grounds of the palace were carefully readied. Women prepared the millet beer pito. The men slaughtered animals for future feasts. The children rehearsed the songs and dances that they would execute.

The real festival commenced with purification rites. The council and the chief would then go to the sacred stool room, where their ancestors' stools were stored in a dark chamber into which very few went. Libation was offered, inviting the ancestors to join the festivities and bestow fertility upon the people during the next year. Most significant would be dressed up in his full ceremonial attire following this ritual—imposing kente cloth, generation-hands-down gold trimmings, and the sword of state as a symbol of his power to dispense justice.

The first day of Akwasidaekese would see the whole town in the palace square. The great drums—the *atumpan*, the *fontomfrom*—would boom, their intricate rhythms carrying messages interpretable to the learned in the drum language. Dancers would dance the old dances, their feet speaking stories of battles won, crops reaped, and knowledge acquired. The chief would move through the gathered crowd, acknowledging his people, their welcomes, playing out the mutual relationship of ruler and ruled.

But Akwasidaekese was not just performance. It was also the day of the *afahyɛ*, the durbar, when the chief would hear reports from his sub-chiefs and counselors, when disputes would be resolved, when public announcements would be made. It was a day of public reckoning, when the chief needed to show that he had ruled well, that people had grown during his reign, that the covenant was still unbroken between him and the ancestors.

At the *afahyɛ*, any individual from the society could go to the chief to complain or petition. This point of access was inviolable. The chief may postpone adjudication, may order inquiry, but he was not able to close his ears to the petition. This institution guaranteed that even the lowliest in the society got a voice, got a means of being heard by the head at the top.

Followed the ceremonial rituals was the feasting. The families would come together and enjoy sumptuous feasts.

Fufu would be pounded, chicken and goat would be prepared in scrumptious groundnut or palm nut soup. There would be jollof rice, waakye, banku, kelewele, and all the other delicacies the community could muster. The feasting was not about consumption but about confirmation of family ties, about sharing abundance, about the promise for even the poorest families to have enough.

There would be music and dance late into the night until dawn. Young women and young men would court and flirt in the presence of elders who supervised over them but did not disapprove of their actions. Friendships would be cemented. Business agreements would be forged. Arranged marriages would take place. The entire community would be united through shared celebration, shared memory, shared culture.

Akwasidaekese was also the occasion when children born a year before were ritually brought into the community. They were escorted in front of the chief, who blessed and symbolically welcomed them as members of the community under his care. The ritual confirmed the chief's role as father of all, with the responsibility for care of even the youngest and most vulnerable members of the community.

The festival was ended by a thanksgiving ceremony in earnest. The chief would make a libation for the last time, thanking the ancestors in gratitude for having watched over them in the previous year, soliciting continued guidance the coming year. The people gathered together would then retort with the customary thanksgiving: "Yɛda ase!" We give thanks!

This was Akwasidaekese as it had been witnessed for centuries in Amansankrom. This was the festival that had united the community in boom and bust, war and peace, colonial atrocities and promises of freedom.

But under Nana Kwaku Bonsam II, even this noble tradition started getting tarnished.

His first Akwasidaekese, in 2005, previewed the trend. The overlord demanded a "modernized" ceremony. He insisted on having hit recording artists flown in from Accra to entertain, in place of some traditional drumming and dancing. He insisted on palm groves ablaze with garish lights and generators powering sound equipment. He insisted on politicians from the central government as guest of honor.

The mother queen protested. "Akwasidaekese is not entertainment," she said to him flatly. "It is sacred ceremony. It is the renewing of our covenant with the ancestors. You cannot place it under the same guidelines as you would for a political rally or a concert."

But the chief overruled her. "Times change, Nana," he said to her with barely contained condescension. "We have to demonstrate to the outside world that Amansankrom is progressive, that we accept modernity even as we honor tradition."

What he was trying to do, even though he did not overtly speak of it, was that he wished to utilize the festival as a platform through which he would cast his own shadow, proclaim his links with influential individuals in Accra, turn

Amansankrom into a soapbox for his own vested interests and not a sacred ground for communal rebirth.

The 2005 festival was costly—much more costly than any of the previous Akwasidaekese. The generators themselves cost more than the total budget of previous festivals. The musicians charged fees that shocked the elders. The guests of honor had to be treated to wine and food in style. And the chief insisted the community foot the bill in special levies and gifts.

Most families were not able to afford these costs. The umbrella ceremony which was meant to be a celebratory occasion turned out to be one of bitterness and dread. People paid because they were afraid of disobeying, not that they thought the costs were fair.

The ceremony itself was an odd combination. The traditional elements did not disappear—libation was poured, the drums of the gods were beaten, the ancestor stools remained prestigious. But mixed among these were the alien and misplaced items. The Accra musicians sang highlife and hiplife songs that had nothing to do with Kwahu custom. The politicians delivered speeches which politicized the *afahyɛ*. The sophisticated lights and sound devices created a carnival-like ambiance which seemed to consecrate the holy light.

And then there was the very first Akwasidaekese of the new chief, the elders withdrew in confidentiality to deliberate on what had occurred. They gathered inside the compound of one of the most elderly elders, men whose lives had known colonialism, independence, and now this tempestuous present.

"This wasn't Akwasidaekese," one of the elders complained. "This was something else. It looked like our festival, it used our festival's name, but the vibe was wrong."

Yet another old man, an octogenarian who had attended over seventy Akwasidaekese ceremonies, spoke in a trembling whisper: "The ancestors were not revered. Yes truly, the libation was made, the words uttered. But it was empty. The chief's heart was not in it. He was posturing, not communing. He was boasting, not serving."

The queen mother, who was also invited to the meeting, heard out the men's grievance sternly. Then she spoke: "What the chief has done to the festival is what he is doing to all of life in our community. He commodifies that which is sacred. He takes the traditions that bind us together and uses them to further his own ends. He takes the power we've given him and distorts it."

"But what can we do?" one of the young elders, a fiftyish man, insisted. "He has the power. He has the politicians in his pocket. If we oppose him openly, he will destroy us."

The queen mother said nothing for a very long time. And then she said something that would be remembered: "Trees that grow too quickly have thin wood. They are beautiful, but they snap in the first cutting wind. The chief has ascended quickly, and he is constructing everything on sand. We must wait. We must record all. We must hold to our ways as best we may, save what we can save, and wait for the inevitable time when his own deeds destroy him."

This was the passive resistance strategy—to keep the traditions, however tainted, in order to keep alive the memory of what they ought to be. Keep records of the corruptions, so that someday there would be a document. Wait patiently, with the patience that comes from the realization that injustice will frequently bear within itself the seeds of its own defeat.

But it was not simple. Each successive Akwasidaekese was more complex, more costly, more tainted. By his third year on the job, the chief had altered the festival so much that it barely resembled the original. The chief had built a special observation deck—he referred to it as the "VIP section"—where he and his dignitary guests could watch the fun from the cool comfort of air conditioning. Accessing the section necessitated special tickets in the chief's possession, which he used as rewards for loyalty and punishment for disobedience.

The ancient right of every citizen to present oneself before the chief during *afahyɛ* was effectively abolished. Petitions were now presented in advance, filtered by the chief's counselors, and only those that were endorsed would be entertained. It was capricious and corrupting—petitions of persons who had bribed or who were favorable to the chief were entertained, but petitions of his detractors were not heard.

The queen mother, even in her role, was progressively pushed to the sidelines throughout the festival. She sat beside the chief in important ceremonies as a symbol of male and female balance in Akan leadership. But Kwaku Bonsam had arranged for her to sit behind, with government officials and successful sponsors taking seats of honor.

Most egregious perhaps was what happened to the holy stool's room. For generations, the room had been kept by the stool keeper, a retired woman who had learned the job from her mother, who had learned it from her mother before her. The stool keeper was responsible for cleaning the stools of the ancestors, for preparing the rituals properly, for keeping the sacred cleanliness of the room.

The village chief replaced the elderly stool keeper, saying that she was too old and the job needed to be "professionalized." In her place, he installed his own relative, a woman who didn't know the traditions and treated the sacred stools as common objects. Worse, he let the tourists—influential visitors whom he was wooing for possible business arrangements—see the stool room for money. The ancestral shrine is now a tourist site, the religious to the commercial.

These developments had the result of filtering into other traditional practices. The child-naming rituals, which had been simple family events with traditional etiquette, became lavish affairs where families felt it was imperative to spend more money than they could without seeming poor or neglectful. Funeral rituals, which had been significant but unostentatious, inflated into costly extravaganzas where families committed themselves to provide their deceased loved ones with "proper" funerals.

This inflation of customary practice placed awful pressure on families. To opt out, to demand simpler ceremonies, was to court accusations of being uncivilized, tossing away tradition, showing disrespect to the ancestors. But to comply meant financial hardship and sustained the chief's stinking system, for many of the spiraling expenses were in the form of fees and payments that lined the chief's and his friends' pockets.

But while traditions were being desecrated at the top, something else was taking place at the bottom. People's family lives were holding on to traditions more closely, as if in retribution for the public debasement. Grandparents were paying more attention to instructing children in the old tales, the proverbs, the correct greeting of elders, the significance of traditional cloth designs and symbols.

Kwame Osei saw it among his students. They were able to recite proverbs memorized from their elders. They memorized clan histories. They had kinship responsibilities with an accuracy that amazed him. As if the society, knowing something important was being lost, was attempting to save it at the family and neighborhood levels.

The mosques and the churches also turned into cultural centers for preservation. The imams and the pastors, while at odds over theology, were concerned that community values were thinning out. They spoke against corruption and greed, but typically in generalities that did not single out the chief. They preached honesty, integrity, and service to the community—speaking against the chief's conduct without ever mentioning his name.

Young people reacted to this messaging in complex forms. Some became cynical, believing that tradition was all about hypocrisy, that adults teaching values did not live them. But others—quite likely the majority—evolved to a sophisticated literacy. They could differentiate between tradition as it ought to be adhered to and tradition corrupted. They grew up, in effect, custodians of an ideal tradition that lived more in memory and hope than reality.

Yaa, the bright pupil who had been introduced to Kwame's documentation book, was interested in customary culture in a different manner. She started interviewing elderly people, recording their stories and memories of how things had been done in the past. She recorded customary rituals on books, attempting to capture knowledge which she was afraid would be lost.

"Why in the world are you doing that?" her mother asked, mystified by her daughter's new fascination with the stories of old people.

"Because someone has to remember," said Yaa practically. "When the chief dies—and he will die one day—someone will have to know how to do things. Someone will have to rebuild what was destroyed."

Her mother gazed at her anxiously and proudly. "Be careful, daughter. The chief dislikes individuals who remember too much."

But Yaa kept going, working quietly and painstakingly. Other youth came to help her who were as interested. They created an unofficial study group which they named "Sankofa"—the Akan phrase for "go back and bring it back," represented by a bird flying ahead but looking back. The name spoke of their mission: to go back and take back knowledge while moving ahead into the future.

The Sankofa folk gathered in a number of homes, always secretly, never mentioning what they did. They learned about the old systems of government, contrasted them with what presently existed, and debated one another as to what ideal leadership would be like. They learned the lost traditional crafts—pottery, weaving, drum-making. They performed traditional dance and song, not to entertain but to learn.

This grassroots cultural preservation action was not planned resistance. Sankofa's youth were not conspiring against the chief to topple him or organize demonstrations. But they were engaging in something perhaps even more potent: holding onto a different vision for what their society might be, keeping alive cultural memory that one day could form the basis for rebirth.

The head, set on more immediate opposition, rejected these cultural pursuits for the most part. He perceived them as innocuous nostalgia, youth frivolities with nothing better to do. He did not know that culture, warehoused and passed on, could be a greater resistance than direct action.

In Kwaku Bonsam's fifth year of rule, Amansankrom existed in a bizarre double life. In the public rituals and official institutions, officially, the dream of the chief for a "modernized" community held sway. Customs were commodified, trimmed down, or dropped. The Akwasidaekese festival was a costly spectacle. Holy places were desecrated. The chief people covenant was ruptured.

But underneath this official reality, there existed a second Amansankrom. In compounds of households, in night gossip, in careful schooling that was transmitted from generation to generation, the actual traditions survived. The tales went on. The lessons were imparted. The remembrance of what the people had once been, and could be again, endured.

It was within this conflict—between the prostitution of official culture and the stubbornness of grassroots tradition—that the seeds of future opposition were planted and grew. The chief might have controlled ceremonies, but he could not command memory. He might have commercialized festivals, but he could not eliminate the awareness of what those festivals had once stood for. He might have pushed the queen mother and the elders apart, but he was unable to destroy the power that they still wielded in people's hearts.

And so, the citizens waited, grasped what they could, clung to what was precious to them, stirred and seethed—though few yet understood it—until the day that the built-up burden of corruption at last became too heavy to endure and something would have to yield.

Chapter 4: Corruption and Chieftaincy Litigation

Amansankrom slowly woke up, like a creature coming out of a deep sleep. Each breath of dawn broke the hold of the night. Even though it looked like everything was fine, the town's peace wasn't really there. It was the quiet before a storm, the false calm that sets in before long-suppressed emotions finally come to the surface. Angry people had been talking about it in whispers in homes and at meetings for months, until it turned into words that were too sharp to ignore.

When the sixth year of Chief Kwaku Bonsam's leadership arrived, those murmurs no longer hid in the dark. Claims of corruption came to light, tarnishing the promise that had once marked his rule.

These were specific and damning accusations. Community members charged that money set aside for the new clinic—money raised through special levies and supplemented by a government grant—had been diverted. The construction of the clinic had gone no further than laying the foundation; the project was abandoned while the chief constructed a palatial new residence for himself on the outskirts of town. The timing was suspicious, the amounts roughly equivalent, and no satisfactory accounting had been provided despite repeated requests from the elders.

Then there were the contracts: repair of roads, renovation of schools, and improvement of the market. Whichever of these community projects came up, it always fell into the hands of the same few contractors, who all had very close ties with the chief. The contractors consistently overcharged and did a poor job, but were never penalized for their failures. Meanwhile, competent local artisans and builders without palace connections were systematically shut out of opportunities.

The harder-to-prove bribery was common. Businesspeople spoke in hushed tones about "consultation fees" required to get permits, "donations" expected before licenses were issued, and "gifts" that smoothed the way for favorable decisions. Applicants who paid saw their requests handled with remarkable efficiency. Those who did not were trapped in an unending cycle of delays, missing files, and inexplicable administrative complications.

"It's not corruption," the smooth-talking young man who was the chief's spokesman, called Kofi Mensah, would say if challenged. "It's the modern way of doing business. The chief must be compensated for his time and expertise. These are administrative fees, perfectly legitimate."

At this point, people knew better; they knew what separated legitimate fees from extortion, reasonable compensation from systematic looting. They knew that as the chief's compound expanded with each passing year, the number of his vehicles multiplied, and his children attended those expensive private schools in Accra, as the community schools lacked even the simplest equipment.

They saw and remembered, and their resentment grew.

Kwame Osei, in his quiet manner, began documenting the allegations with meticulous care, just as he had once chronicled the erosion of old customs. He recorded every complaint, every vanished fund, every suspicious contract. The pages of his record book slowly formed a ledger of corruption that he hoped would one day speak for itself.

"You're playing at a dangerous game," his wife warned one evening as she watched him writing by the light of the lamp. "If the chief discovers what you're up to—"

"Then he finds it," Kwame said in a very calm voice, while his hands shook a little as he wrote. "Someone has to remember. Someone has to be a witness. If not me, who?"

The allegations of corruption carried weight, though they were only one thread in Amansankrom's unraveling story. The greater struggle lay in the question of the stool itself and whether Kwaku Bonsam had ever rightfully earned it. That dispute, once confined to whispers and petitions, had now become a fierce contest that risked breaking the town's fragile peace.

Prince Akwasi Appiah was a quiet, scholarly man in his early fifties, living in Kumasi when Kwaku Bonsam came into the stool. Akwasi taught history in a secondary school, as he was far more comfortable with books than with politics. However, he, too, was from the royal lineage through his mother's line— proper matrilineal succession, according to Akan custom—and many felt his claim to the stool was stronger than Kwaku Bonsam's.

"The problem," one of the elders supporting Akwasi explained, "is that Kwaku Bonsam's mother, though of royal blood, was from a junior branch of the family. Tradition holds that her son should not have been considered for the stool when candidates from the senior branch were available. But when the selection was made, Akwasi was away in Kumasi, attending to his dying father. By the time he returned and learned what had happened, Kwaku Bonsam had already been installed."

Akwasi Appiah's supporters maintained that the entire process had been engineered to keep him from the stool. They claimed that the queen mother and the kingmakers had been swayed by influence or money to favor Kwaku Bonsam. To them, the skipped rituals and the hurried conclusion were proof enough that tradition had been compromised.

"It was not just wrong," insisted Nana Yaa Asantewaa, a high-ranking queen mother from a neighboring town who took up Akwasi's cause. "It was a violation of everything our traditions stand for. Chieftaincy is not to be seized through trickery and manipulation. It has to be earned through lineage and character, and proper observance of custom."

Supporters of Chief Kwaku Bonsam told a different story. To them, his selection had been entirely legitimate. He was born into a recognized royal lineage, and the kingmakers, they insisted, had followed every required step of tradition. Akwasi's claims, according to them, were only inspired by jealousy and wounded pride. Akwasi was a bitter man who could not come to terms with the fact that somebody else had been chosen over him.

"Akwasi Appiah had his chance," one of the chief's most loyal councilors said recently at a public gathering. "He was away when the selection was made. That's not our fault. The kingmakers cannot wait forever. The town needed a leader, and they chose the best candidate available. If Akwasi cannot accept that, then his quarrel is with tradition itself, not with Chief Kwaku Bonsam."

The tension surrounding the chieftaincy claim eventually reached a point where quiet negotiation no longer seemed possible. Encouraged by influential allies and elders from neighboring communities, Akwasi Appiah moved to confront the matter through official channels. He filed a case before the Regional House of Chiefs, aiming to unseat Kwaku Bonsam and assert his own right to lead.

The litigation had started three years ago, by which time it had seen mountains of money and reams of paperwork expended by both parties. The Regional House of Chiefs listened to kingmakers, elders, genealogists, and traditional authorities; it examined family trees, reviewed historical precedents, and debated fine points of custom and law.

But no decision had been reached. The case was complex, the evidence conflicting, the customs themselves interpretable. Each side could mount a vigorous argument, replete with its experts and authorities; each side could cite precedents that endorsed its view. And so the litigation dragged on, year after year, with no resolution in sight.

It is this chieftaincy dispute that has fractured Amansankrom along fault lines, cutting across families and neighborhoods, with brothers pitted against one another, each supporting a different claimant, and lifelong friends estranged through arguments about succession and legitimacy. Where the town should have been united, it was divided against itself.

The followers of Chief Kwaku Bonsam saw themselves as defenders of the established order, protectors of stability against chaos. They maintained that allowing the destooling of Chief Bonsam would set a precedent whereby any disgruntled rival can start litigation against an installed chief, plunging chieftaincy into endless uncertainty.

"Today it is Akwasi Appiah," argued one, "tomorrow another one, and the day after, another. Where do we stop? We cannot have a system where chiefs are being challenged now and then removed. There must be respect for decisions made by those who hold power, even if we disagree."

Akwasi's followers viewed the situation through a different lens. They believed the chieftaincy was not being undermined but restored to its rightful order. To them, this correction of a deep injustice was precisely what preserved the integrity of their traditional institutions. Allowing Kwaku Bonsam's dubious elevation, they insisted, would set an even more dangerous precedent: chieftaincy can be secured through gerrymandering and is not a matter of proper succession.

"If we allow this to continue, then we are saying that tradition does not matter, and the rules can be bent by whoever has the most influence or money. Is that the message we want to send to future generations?" said an advocate for Akwasi.

That placed the queen mother of Amansankrom in a very painful position. She was a party to the selection of Kwaku Bonsam, though with much reluctance, and there were now questions over whether she had indeed been coerced or duped. Some Akwasi supporters saw her as an accomplice in the questionable selection process, while to others, she herself had been manipulated.

Privately, however, Queen Mother had her misgivings. "I don't know anymore," she had confided in a close friend. "At the time, I thought we were doing the right thing. The kingmakers convinced me that the procedure was sound and that Kwaku Bonsam's bloodline was beyond dispute. I accepted their word and allowed the matter to move forward. With hindsight, I recognize the clues I ignored—the speed, the pressure, and the deliberate avoidance of uncomfortable inquiries. I am afraid we may have made a terrible mistake."

But all of this, she could say only in private. For her, admitting the mistake in public meant more than personal embarrassment. It meant shaking the moral ground on which tradition stood. Such an admission would have hinted that even the queen mother and the kingmakers could be influenced or deceived. Hence, she kept quiet, not fully defending the chief while not openly supporting his rival, treading a tightrope precariously between opposing camps.

This was further compounded by the already complex issue of land litigation, arguably the most volatile source of conflict in Amansankrom. The town was not new to land disputes; indeed, such disputes had been a perennial bone of contention in many communities throughout Ghana. During Chief

Kwaku Bonsam's regime, however, land litigation reached unprecedented levels, propelled by the chief's systematic manipulation of traditional land-tenure systems for personal gain.

Put briefly, the problem was that land under Akan customary law was held in common rather than individually. The chief was custodian of the communal lands held in trust for the people and presided over their distribution in accordance with traditional practice. However, although individual families might be granted use rights over specific portions passed on through successive generations, the ultimate ownership of such land lay with the community, as represented by the chief.

It was, essentially, a rather good system because it functioned reasonably well for many centuries, depending on the chief exercising his custodial role with integrity and fairness. In Kwaku Bonsam's hands, however, it had become a vehicle of personal enrichment and political control.

The charges were many and grave: it was said that the chief had appropriated some of the best tracts of communal lands and rewarded his loyalists and cronies at the expense of the families that for generations had farmed those lands. Further to that, he was accused of selling those pieces of land to outside investors, such as developers from Accra who wanted to build commercial properties, without consultation or fair compensation to the families holding traditional use rights.

Most egregiously, the chief was accused of falsifying documentation to support his land transactions by creating false historical records that showed certain communal lands as his personal family property and hence free to be sold as he saw fit.

"My grandfather farmed that land," said one elderly farmer, shaking with anger and grief as he spoke to the circle of concerned community members around him. "His father farmed it before him. We have worked that soil for over a hundred years. And now the chief says it is not ours, we have no rights to it, and he has sold it to some businessman from the capital who wants to build a hotel. Where is the justice in that?"

It was a land dispute that had triggered the litigation cascade, wherein families filed cases against the chief in traditional courts to protect their ancestral lands, while the chief counterfiled a claim that the land in question had never belonged to them, that they were squatters with no legitimate claims. Outside investors who had been caught in the middle also filed their own legal actions, seeking clarity on the ownership of the lands they had bought in good faith.

The government institution responsible for resolving such disputes, the Regional Lands Commission, soon found itself overwhelmed by the number of cases presented from Amansankrom. Files piled up, hearings were scheduled months or even years in advance, and no clear resolutions emerged. A legal system that was never exceptionally efficient at its best ground almost to a standstill under the weight of competing claims and counterclaims.

Meanwhile, in Amansankrom, land disputes had bred a climate of fear and insecurity. Families who had farmed their lands peacefully for years were finding themselves facing eviction. Young people were being told that the family parcels on which they hoped to build homes had been sold out from under them. Farmers who considered investing in cocoa trees or other crops that take years to mature put their plans on hold, uncertain about whether they would own the land at harvest time.

The disputes also provided avenues for violence: in several cases, the chief supporters had tried to force families off the disputed lands; scuffles took place; crops on the farms were destroyed, houses damaged, and one young farmer was seriously injured in one gruesome incident in a clash with the chief's enforcers.

"This is where corruption ultimately leads," Kwame Osei wrote in his record book. "It starts off with misappropriated funds and irregular contracts. But eventually, it comes down to violence, to people driven from their ancestral lands, to families torn apart. The greed of the chief has poisoned everything it touches."

It is at this juncture, with all crises converging—allegations of corruption, litigation over chieftaincy, and land disputes— that this perfect storm overwhelms Amansankrom. Each problem feeds into others, amplifying them and creating a web of conflict for which there appears to be no solution in sight.

These corruption allegations tarnished the chief's moral authority and, thus, his suitability to act as a disinterested arbiter of the land disputes. The chieftaincy litigation raised questions about his legal right to apportion the land in the first place, if he was not the true chief, as all of his land deals could be declared null and void. The land dispute created resources that fueled both corruption and litigation: the chief needed ever more money to pay lawyers and buy off opponents.

With the seventh anniversary of the chief's rise to power at hand, the standoff in the town was complete. The Regional House of Chiefs was no nearer to a resolution of the chieftaincy dispute. There had been no investigation into the widely believed corruption allegations, let alone any charges. Land litigation multiplied many times faster than the courts could handle, resulting in a backlog that would take several years to clear.

Life in Amansankrom went on, strangely divided between appearance and reality. The chief's court and the palace continued their pageantry, maintaining the illusion of harmony. Beneath that façade, in quiet talks, in Osei's careful notes, and in the growing circles of the Sankofa youth, resistance gathered strength day by day.

They bend toward one another, voices trembling like wind through leaves. From lip to lip passes the same question, ancient and unanswerable: "How long? How long shall we bear this pain?"

None of them knew it, though the signs were already there. The moment of rupture was closer than anyone dared to believe. It was as if the accumulated weight of corruption, illegitimacy, and injustice became insupportable. The chief's administration projected an image of stability and power. In truth, its base was loose and unsteady, built on compromise and fear. The moment real pressure was applied, the foundation sank, and the entire structure began to collapse.

The people gathered more frequently now—in homes and courtyards, in churches, and in the market square once the day's trade was done. Their voices, low and careful, turned toward shared grievances and the faint hope of change. The idea of action still felt distant and perilous, yet with every passing day, it seemed a little more possible.

"We cannot just wait and wait," one young community leader insisted in a late 2011 meeting. "There is a place for the elders' strategy of patient documentation. However, at a certain point, we must act. At some point, we have to rise up and demand justice."

The same question always followed their talk, quiet but insistent. How could change actually begin? "The chief has the politicians behind him. He has money, enforcers, and legal resources. What do we have?"

"We have the truth," Yaa said, leading this Sankofa group. The quiet work of cultural preservation had made her bold, had given her a deep understanding of what Amansankrom had been and might be again. "We have the traditions—the real traditions, not corrupted versions of them that the chief puts forward. We have the memory of how things should be done. And we have each other—if we find the courage to stand together."

It was a stirring sentiment, and one with which many who heard it could only agree. Still, as all knew, courage was easier to summon in principle than in practice. The chief had shown time and again that he did not take kindly to opposition. Those who dissented from his view lost business, were denied communal amenities, and were harassed by the chief's supporters. So far, nobody had been seriously hurt, but the threat of violence hung heavy in the air, like humidity before a storm.

These murmurs of resistance were bound to reach the queen mother. Torn between hope and fear, she hoped perhaps that at last the community might find strength to right the wrongs that had been committed. Yet, she felt that premature action was likely to result in violence and chaos, that the cure might prove worse than the disease.

One evening, she gathered some elders together at her compound: men and women she trusted, dedicated individuals who, over the years, had served selflessly in a balance of tradition and pragmatism.

She whispered to them, "The time is coming, I don't know precisely when, but it feels like it. There comes a time, building up to that pressure, when something has to give. We must be prepared: we have to think seriously of the next step ahead, finding our way to harness this discontent into constructive change, not destructive conflict."

The elders nodded gravely; they, too, could feel the crisis at hand. They wondered how to protect their town from the storm that was forming around it. Others had tried and failed, leaving behind only ruin and grief. The path to survival was unclear, and no one trusted that calm words alone would be enough.

"We need to strengthen the alternatives," one said, an older man whose insight into conflict resolution was well recognized. "Not just oppose the chief, but bring a clear vision of what proper leadership looks like. Show people that there is another way, a better way, solidly based on true tradition rather than its corruption."

"And we need to build bridges," said another. "Even amongst the chief's supporters, there are people who feel uncomfortable with what he is doing but feel trapped by their previous allegiances. We need to make it possible for them to change sides without losing face, to join the movement for reform without feeling they're betraying their earlier commitments."

The guidance was both measured and practical. In the difficult days to come, success would depend on restraint and thoughtful coordination. Unity among those seeking change would be the surest strength they could possess. But unity, as people in Amansankrom were learning, may well be the scarcest resource of all in a town divided against itself.

As the meeting broke up and the elders disappeared into the night, the queen mother sat in her compound under the stars, which had witnessed the rise and fall of so many generations of chiefs. The weight of tradition, the sacred trust that had just been violated, the community she loved, the future so uncertain that it had to be withheld—all these flashed through her mind.

She prayed in the quiet rhythm her elders had taught her long ago. "Give us wisdom," she murmured, "courage when the moment calls for it, patience when restraint is needed, and the sense to tell them apart." The words gathered strength as she went on. "Carry us through the storm ahead. Let your will be done, and may our people come through with their unity, their customs, and their pride intact."

Chief Kwaku Bonsam sat in the comfort of his compound, the steady hum of the air conditioner filling the stillness. A folder of new intelligence rested before him. His informers had done their work well, and every page carried fragments of what was happening beyond his walls. He knew about the meetings, the whispered conversations, the budding resistance. Yet he was secure in his power, sure he could weather any storm.

"They are just complainers," he told Kofi Mensah, his spokesman. "Every chief has somebody who opposes him. Every leader has their critics. They'll talk and grumble, but ultimately they'll do nothing. They lack the cohesion and the guts to seriously take me on." He nodded, but to himself, he wasn't so sure.

There were subtle shifts in mood in this town, a hardening of resolve amongst people who hitherto had been passive. However, he kept such thoughts to himself, as the chief did not like to hear bad news, and Kofi valued his position far too much to risk its loss with unwelcome observations.

The town waited with a patience that no longer felt peaceful. Ledgers were updated, the Sankofa group widened its circle, and the courts dragged on with cases no one expected to end. Beneath the routines of daily life, frustration thickened, rising like heat beneath stone, preparing to burst. The stillness that settled over Amansankrom was unlike any peace the people had known. It was the silence that comes before a cry, the quiet of hearts that sense a trial approaching. Every man, every woman felt it in their bones—the inevitability of something vast and merciless drawing near.

The questions of time and fate haunted their sleep: when would it come, and who among them would remain whole after it passed? Beneath that dense and trembling calm, the town waited, breath held, soul burdened, for the storm to claim its hour.

Chapter 5: The Role of Women in Amansankrom

Nana Adwoa got out of bed at the crack of dawn, the mist hanging still over the verdant hillsides above Amansankrom. Her mountain home was illuminated by the gentle dawn light, which prompted her to get moving. She fell into rhythm with the needs of her family in Amansankrom. It was an ancient choreography set by the universe and taught her by her mother and her mother's mother before her, reaching back through generations to a time beyond memory.

She started with the compound, sweeping it clean with the long fronds of a palm, the soft swishing a gentle prelude to the town's awakening. Left to right, forward, and back, the motion was meditative, clearing away yesterday's detritus and making room for today's possibilities. It was simple work, menial perhaps in other people's estimation, yet symbolic as well: a clean compound meant an orderly household, a family respectful of itself and its neighbors.

She went to the stream in the town called Kapari to fetch the day's water when she had finished sweeping. The eldest daughter joined in fetching water from the stream with large clay pots. The mother and daughter made their way up the path to the stream, singing Aseda, a song of gratitude. Their voices joined the morning chorus of birds, and the whisper of leaves stirred by the wind. The path to Kapari was smooth— smoothened by the countless feet of generations of women who, before the crowing of the first cockerel, had made that journey, borne similar clay pots upon their heads, and sung similar songs.

The women of Amansankrom met by the stream in the cool of the morning. They washed, scrubbed, and talked as their songs drifted through the mist. Their work bound them together, turning routine into quiet communion.

They filled their pots quickly, their movements sure and measured. Each woman balanced her load on her head with the quiet confidence of long habit. The water, drawn from mountain springs, was clear and cold, sustaining the rhythm of life in every house.

Within minutes, they were done with that morning's job, and Akua Safoa, leaving her mother, went behind the house, where she tended her small backyard garden. The rich soil cooled and dampened Akua Safoa's fingers simultaneously as she tended to the lines of food crops she had planted. The labor demanded strength and endurance, yet it stood at the heart of a woman's duty. The crops she tended fed her family and ensured their survival. The portion left beyond their needs was sold, bringing life and movement to the town's market square.

The garden was the domain of Akua Safoa: small but well-tended. The mainstays of all the meals included cassava and plantain, garden eggs and peppers, okra, and tomatoes. Her mother taught her the secrets of the land—the right crops for each season and how to arrange them in perfect balance. She learned to watch the soil, to sense its needs. In time, she could look at the sky and know exactly when to sow and when to reap. Such knowledge wasn't written in books but was encoded in the memory and practice passed down through demonstration and repetition until it became second nature.

Men worked the plantations and managed the cocoa trade that fed the town's economy. Their contribution was public and widely acknowledged. The women's toil, though hidden from sight, remained the unseen strength on which the community depended. The women tend the food crops so vital for day-to-day living.

This order of work had ancient roots and followed the matrilineal laws of Akan society. Women were seen as the source from which all life flowed and through whom family lines endured. Their role in providing food carried the sacred weight of sustaining that continuity. A man might grow wealthy from cocoa, but he would go hungry without the food his wife and daughters produced. This was understood by all, even if rarely said.

She woke early, made breakfast in the kitchen: stewed garden eggs and the first meal of the day. The aroma filled the air, announcing that soon it would be time to converge, eat, talk, and start off, nourished adequately in body and spirit. The kitchen mirrored the garden in its meaning and its order. It was the woman's space, where she shaped raw things into nourishment. There, her attention and love found their most practical expression.

She had fed her family and was getting ready for the markets in town. She had a keen head for numbers and a sharper one for people. In the marketplace, her word carried weight, and her dealings brought steady profit. The income she earned sustained her home and strengthened her standing in the community. It was in the marketplace that the true economic power of women revealed itself.

The surplus from their farms turned into cash beneath the shade of market stalls. Their skill in bargaining and trade often decided the prosperity of their families. She stood at the edge of the marketplace, surveying the chaos. The air was thick with the sounds of bartering. Beside her, her daughter, Akua Safoa, sat patiently, a basket of ripe mangoes carefully placed beside her.

At seventeen, Akua was beginning to rival her mother's looks—a fact to which Nana Adwoa was both pleased and unsettled all at once. A woman's beauty stood as both privilege and trial. In a world that watched too closely, it became a double-edged gift. It offered her opportunity, yet it also marked her as vulnerable to the gaze and will of others.

"Akua," Nana Adwoa said in a low tone, "the fruit is sweet, yet the foolish trader gives it away for nothing." Akua laughed and nodded, clear about what her mother was driving at and the lesson that came with it. These were lessons learned at her mother's knee, not only about trading but about life itself, regarding value and worth, knowing when to stand firm and when to compromise. Nana Adwoa had taught her to bargain fiercely, to spot a counterfeit coin by touch, and to maintain a reputation for honesty that was as valuable as any asset.

In the truest sense, the marketplace belonged to the women of Amansankrom. The men might plant cacao, fell timber, or build homes and roads, but the true heartbeat of the town lay in the women's trade. Through their hands, life and livelihood continued to flow. They sold produce, cloth and clothing, household goods, prepared foods, herbal medicines, and a wide range of other essentials. Women dominated the retail trade, setting prices through collective bargaining, extending credit to regular customers, and managing the complex web of debts and obligations that comprised the local economy.

This economic power soon translated into household influence: usually and often, the successful market woman, like Nana Adwoa, earned more than her husband did, commanded considerable assets, and typically made all significant decisions about family expenditures. The stereotype of the submissive African woman had little basis in Amansankrom, where economic independence provided leverage in household negotiations and community affairs.

Akua watched this all day, as her mother haggled with every man that crossed her path to have her lower the prices of her wares. The men raised their voices in attempts at overpowering her, but Nana Adwoa stood firm. Her wit was sharper than a machete, and she knew the goods she was selling were worth every penny. She matched them word for word, proverb for proverb, never raising her voice, yet never yielding on the essentials either.

As she used to say to one insistent haggler: "You want to eat good mangoes, but pay bad prices. The tree doesn't grow fruit for free, and neither do I sell my labor for free. Pay what is fair or buy from someone else who will cheat you with inferior goods."

He grumbled but paid her asking price, knowing as everybody did that Nana Adwoa's reputation for quality was well-deserved: her mangoes were always full and ripe; she would not sell spoiled goods or short-weight her measures. Honesty, in the long run, proved more profitable than trickery—a lesson that Nana Adwoa herself had learned, one that she was firmly set on passing on to her daughter.

On their walk home afterward, Akua turned to her with a burst of exasperation: "Why do we always have to prove ourselves at every turn, Mama? Why do we have to fight for what rightfully belongs to us?" It was the question of a young person, born of that impatience that comes from seeing injustice but not yet understanding its deeper roots.

Nana Adwoa smiled, her eyes reflecting an expression of weariness mixed with wisdom. "Our strength is not in the fighting of their wars, Akua, but in winning our own. We are the rocks they build their homes on. We are the keepers of the bloodline, the weavers of the future."

She insisted that the men had the formal powers—the chieftaincy, the council of elders, and the public offices—but that behind the scenes, the reins were really held by the women: they controlled the household and the purse strings, and were held in high esteem for their wisdom and adeptness at managing family affairs. The abusuapanyin, the head of the household, might be male in title, but he would be a fool to make major decisions without consulting his wife, his mother, and his sisters. And when it came to issues like marriage, education, property, and inheritance, women's opinions often carried a lot of weight, even though they weren't often heard in public.

Nana Adwoa said, "One day, Akua, you will be a mother and shall have a daughter of your own. Remember the mangoes when that day comes. You are the source of her wealth, and it is your duty to teach her how to protect and nurture it. The best men know this and respect their wives' counsel. This is our inheritance, Akua, not just land or money but wisdom to build a legacy that will last."

Akua no longer saw her mother not as an industrious trader but as the fierce guardian of her family's future. Then she saw what her path demanded of her. It was not a battle of noise or protest, but one of quiet mastery, guided by thought, courage, and dignity. It lay not in her hands but in her heart and mind to pass on to the forthcoming generation of women coming after her.

The women of Amansankrom showed a consistent truth about power. Those who earned their own income held greater sway in their homes and in public affairs. They were partners in shaping destiny, not subjects of it. In this, the matrilineal institution gives force to the way in which they are positioned at the center of kinship networks, the conduits through which property and identity flow across generations.

But women's power did not stop at economics and kinship: from there, it flowed into governance and decision-making, albeit less visibly and formally. The queen mother held an officially recognized position of authority. She balanced the chief's power with her own influence and ensured that the voices of women were heard. On the traditional council, she stood as their representative and guardian. Beyond that formal role, however, lay a variety of informal mechanisms through which women played their part in the governance of the community.

One avenue of mobilization ran through women's associations. Organized around shared economic interests, religious affiliation, or simply proximity within a neighborhood, these groups made it possible for women to come together in discussions of community issues. They enabled them to take a common position and to coordinate collective action. A decision of the women's association was not one to be taken lightly: what women supported or opposed was ultimately to succeed or fail through their control of household resources and through influence with husbands, brothers, or sons.

Over the years, market women at Amansankrom coalesced into quite a formidable union. From their midst emerged a forceful woman in her sixties who had traded for over four decades to lead the association and negotiate with its suppliers, arbitrate disagreements between traders, establish unofficial price ranges, and speak with one voice for the interests of the market women to the chief and town council. In short, even the chief had to listen when the market women spoke as one.

"We are the ones feeding this town," Nana Ama Serwaa had told Chief Kwaku Bonsam to his face, on one occasion when he had proposed an increase in the market fees without consultation. "You may sit on the stool, but we sit on the money. Try squeezing us too hard, and you'll find that money has a way of disappearing." The chief retreated, backing down and negotiating a more reasonable fee structure.

Another avenue of possibility for women in decision-making could be found in the family council. When a major decision faced the family, such as matters of marriage, property, or disputes among members of the extended household, a council would be summoned. Both men and women took part in these discussions, each voice heard according to standing and experience. Older women held influence through age, wisdom, and their deep knowledge of family history and relationships.

It is these councils where women's voices were listened to and their opinions valued. The opinion of a grandmother concerning a proposed marriage is taken seriously. The testimony of a woman concerning property boundaries or of a claim of inheritance was authoritative. This fiction of men making the decisions while the women keep silent does not square with how decisions were made in Amansankrom.

In the late afternoon, the women gathered again, as naming the newborn child to one of the highly regarded families was one of the most significant events to take place in the community. Nana Adwoa, leading the women in a dance that was once graceful and strong, told all present once more that a woman's role is considered one of great strength and resilience, a keeper of tradition, a nurturer of life, and thus an essential pillar to Amansankrom.

This was not a dance in the sense of entertainment. It was a ritual, a prayer, a physical expression of continuity from past to present. The steps had been danced by ancestors and would be danced by descendants, connecting all the women of Amansankrom across time in a single unbroken chain. They personified, in their dance, strength, fertility, endurance—all those qualities that had enabled their people to survive centuries of change and upsets.

With all this power and influence comes a unique set of burdens that the women of Amansankrom have to bear, many of which are not shared by men. In fact, it is the very same matrilineal system that confers centrality on them in the kinship network, which imposes heavy expectations and responsibilities on them.

These were indeed weighty responsibilities weighing at times beyond endurance, particularly during funerals and mourning rites. Like all of the women, Nana Adwoa was obliged to mourn and wail publicly; for the most part, men were exempt. This perhaps was the most critical moment in time for the women culturally and psychologically, in times of mass grief.

In Amansankrom, funerals lasted several days, and the cost in terms of time, money, and psychic energy was enormous. Women were summoned to mourn aloud, to make their pain visible in the presence of others. Their tears and cries stood as proof of devotion and reverence for the departed. The men bore their sorrow in silence, showing strength through control rather than expression.

The ritual of mourning was tiring and often felt performative. Nana Adwoa had cried at dozens of funerals for close relatives, distant kin, neighbors, and respected members of the community. At times, her sorrow ran deep. At other times, it came only from obligation rather than emotion. No matter how she felt, she was expected to play her part, adding her tears to the chorus of mourning that honored the dead and comforted the living.

"Why are we the ones always crying?" her younger sister Akosua once asked in bitterness, following a particularly draining funeral service. "Why do we always show our pain out front while the men stand around like they don't feel anything?"

"Because we carry life," Nana Adwoa had said, "and so we must also carry death. We are the ones who welcome children into the world, and so we must be the ones to bid farewell when they leave it. It may not be fair, perhaps, but it is our role."

But aside from this emotional labor of mourning, other challenges were also at play. A double standard in behavior and reputation was ever-present in women's lives. A man could drink, could be promiscuous, could be loud and boisterous without too much damage to his standing in the community. A woman who did likewise would be condemned as shameful, bringing disgrace on her family in violation of the standards of respectability governing female conduct.

This double standard was most poignantly felt by young women, such as Akua Safoa, who were making their way from girlhood into womanhood against a backdrop where one wrong move could carry implications far into the future. Akua had to be circumspect in the way she attired herself, with whom she spoke, where she went, and how she conducted herself when out in public. Her reputation was fragile, easily damaged by gossip or accusation, and once lost, it was almost impossible to restore completely.

"A man can make a hundred mistakes and still find a good wife," Nana Adwoa had warned her daughter, "but a woman who makes even one mistake may find that no respectable man will have her. It is not fair, but it is reality. Guard your reputation as you would guard gold, because it is more valuable and more easily stolen."

Women were the leading carriers of responsibility for household harmony. If men were the formal heads of households, women were the mediators, the peacemakers—those responsible for smoothing over conflicts, maintaining relationships, and doing the invisible emotional labor involved in managing feelings, anticipating needs, and avoiding disputes.

Nana Adwoa spent untiring hours mediating quarreling relatives and counseling troubled neighbors, keeping together the complex web of relationships that held the extended family together. All this was exhausting work that never ended, rarely acknowledged, and generated no income, yet consumed vast reserves of time and energy. The criticism that a woman would be careless or inadequate in her responsibilities would follow if she failed in her position, but this was to be expected.

During the tenure of Chief Kwaku Bonsam, women suffered from additional pressures: the traditional protection was being gradually eroded while new forms of exploitation started to appear. The chief's corruption had deepened until bribes and personal ties carried more weight than ability or justice. Women often found themselves excluded, disadvantaged by a structure built to serve men and their networks.

These levies and other fees imposed by the chief on the market women were discriminatory, and those who did not yield to bribes were being harassed and obstructed. The women's leader, Nana Ama Serwaa, had been summoned several times to the palace and made to offer cash "contributions" as a quid pro quo for lenient treatment of market women. Refusing to play along, the chief's agents began harassing inspections, issuing threats of closing down stalls for minor infractions, thereby creating fear and uncertainty.

"He tries to intimidate us in order to subjugate us," she tells the women of the market gathered around her. "He knows we are powerful—that we control resources he wants to access—and so he tries to break us down, to make us dependent on his favor rather than confident in our rights."

The spate of land disputes that mushroomed during the chief's tenure fell disproportionately on the women. This often extracted the heaviest toll on women, who were now being dispossessed of their ancestral lands. Gardens they had tended for years were destroyed, the small businesses they had created near family compounds dislocated, and the security that came from knowing they had land to fall back on—land to grow food, land to build a house, land to pass on to their children—evaporated.

Because women held use rights generally through male relatives, not in their own name, this put them in a particularly vulnerable position should disputes arise. A woman whose husband or brother sold family land without proper consultation had little legal redress. Community oversight and family consensus at least afforded some protection for women's interests in the traditional system of land tenure, but manipulation by the chief left them exposed and vulnerable.

Domestic violence rose not as some product of the chief's corruption but rather simply because economic stress and social breakdown created more volatile households: men humiliated by their failures in the new economy took frustrations out on wives and daughters as mounting debts overwhelmed them and expectations were dashed. Community institutions that had traditionally intervened in such cases—the family councils, the elders, and the chief's court—functioned less well now as trust in formal authority eroded.

"Where do we go for justice?" one woman, whose face was bruised from the beating by her husband, asked in a meeting with members of the women's association. "The court of the chief does not take our complaints seriously. The elders are afraid to act. Even our own families, at times, tell us to be patient, to endure, and not to make trouble. Are we to just accept this?"

It was a question to which there was no easy answer. The protections that had long guarded the well-being of women had fallen away. The queen mother's voice carried less weight, family councils were ignored, and the chief no longer acted as a guardian of justice. Under Kwaku Bonsam's leadership, corruption replaced integrity. Women navigated a more perilous and unpredictable world, where sources of protection and support were fewer and less reliable.

The women of Amansankrom lived under the weight of injustice, yet they did not yield to despair. Each day, they found within themselves a stubborn will to survive. They gathered in secret, shared what they could, and wove their endurance into quiet acts of courage. The women's associations also took on more explicit political forms than before, extending their traditional preoccupation with economic interests to wider questions of governance and justice.

The coalition of women's groups started maintaining a parallel record with Kwame Osei of abuses and exploitations, ranging from domestic violence to property fraud perpetrated against women and harassment of market women by the chief's agents. It was both a historical record and supported legal cases, and it proved to the women that they were not alone.

The queen mother, certain that the situation was worsening, began holding regular councils with representatives of the women's associations. The gatherings gave them a forum to express their concerns and to plan their next steps. Through these exchanges, a quiet but steady resolve began to take form. Through her rank, the queen mother offered the women both protection and credibility in their struggle. She lent her name to their cause, knowing how far it could reach and where it must stop. Her power was real, but so were the boundaries that confined it.

"We must be like water," the queen mother told one gathering. "Water is soft and yields to pressure, but over time, it wears away even the hardest stone. We can't confront the chief's power directly—not yet. But we can erode it, slowly and steadily, through our collective refusal to cooperate with injustice."

This quiet resistance strategy was perhaps best exemplified by the market women's reaction to the chief's demands for increased fees. Rather than refuse, which would undoubtedly have brought retaliation, they began an organized form of passive resistance. Market women started closing their stalls early, pleading sickness or family obligations. They reduced their stock so that business would appear slow and therefore unable to stand higher fees. They extended credit more liberally to customers, reducing their cash on hand and therefore their ability to pay fees.

These were techniques that were subtle enough that the chief could not respond with direct punishment, yet effective enough that his revenue from market fees fell dramatically. He knew he was being resisted, and yet he couldn't quite prove it, or stop it. The market women had turned their apparent weakness, their fragmented structure and dependence on daily trade, into a strength in the development of a resistance that was impossible to identify and impossible to suppress without destroying the market itself.

The young women, such as Yaa and Akua Safoa, are finding new ways to self-assert themselves, claiming space for their voices. Though focused on cultural preservation, the Sankofa group was also predominantly female in its membership and leadership. Rather than waiting for change, these young women actively prepared themselves to become agents of such change.

Yaa had emerged as an increasingly articulate voice among the youth. Work documenting traditional practices had given her a deep understanding of how things should be done, and she was by no means bashful about pointing out when current practices deviated from tradition. She spoke at gatherings, wrote articles for a small newsletter circulated among educated youth, and organized workshops on traditional governance and women's roles.

"They have shown us the way to be strong through examples," Yaa tells one gathering of young women. "They have survived colonization, independence, economic crisis, and now this corrupt chief," she says. "They have maintained their dignity and power in the face of all attempts by the system to diminish them. We must learn from them, but also go further. We must not just survive, we must transform. We must not just resist, we must rebuild."

But perhaps the most powerful form of resistance lay here: through generational continuity, elder women passed on knowledge and strategies to the younger women, who, from that base, developed new strategies. The women in a single generation may not have achieved significant change, but the next generation was poised to pick up the fight.

Churches and mosques also played significant roles in supporting women and taking their concerns seriously. In most religiously active communities, the majority of participants were women, and for those pastors or imams who sought to maintain their influence, taking women's concerns seriously was thus unavoidable. Sermons increasingly took up issues of domestic violence, economic justice, and responsibilities of leadership, affording a religious sanction to women's resistance against abuse and exploitation.

Examples include: Presbyterian Women's Fellowship, Methodist Women's Movement, and Muslim Women's Association. The women's groups provided both material and spiritual strength. They ran rotating credit schemes that sustained families and used their meetings to confront local issues in ways that tied faith to daily responsibility.

"God did not create women to be doormats," one popular woman pastor preached in a fellowship meeting for women. "He created us to be co-creators—partners in the work of building a just society. When we see injustice, when we experience abuse, when we are denied our rights, we are not just defending ourselves. We are defending the order that God intended for the world."

These are powerful messages that resonated in the minds and hearts of women socialized to submit, yet conscious at the same time of the fact that submission to injustice did not equate with faithfulness to God. Sometimes religion, apparently legitimizing women's subordination, was reclaimed as a source of empowerment and resistance.

Assuming this position of relative economic power in 2012, women of Amansankrom maintain influence in household and kinship networks, organize for protection, and resist exploitation. Still, they knew how fragile such protections could be and how quickly traditional safeguards could crumble under corrupt leadership. They also felt the weight of vulnerability within a system that granted formal authority to men while expecting women to preserve its stability.

Whether this frequently invisible, yet potent force of women could or would be mobilized effectively in support of systemic change would be tested in the approaching confrontation with Chief Kwaku Bonsam. Would market women apply economic leverage to compel accountability? Would women's associations coordinate their actions with the broader resistance movement? Would young women, like Yaa, take on leading roles in creating and building a better future? Would the Queen Mother use moral authority to legitimate opposition and protect dissidents?

These were questions to be answered in the months ahead, but one thing was clear: the women were not going to go along as passive observers in this struggle. They had invested too much in their families and communities and had too much at stake to continue putting up with continued corruption and exploitation in silence.

Or, to put it another way, the question was whether they could translate that power from diffuse and informal to focused and effective. How well did they succeed in moving from individual strategies of survival to collective action? Were they able to claim not just influence but authority, not just economic independence but political voice? Answers would come in due time amidst an unfolding crisis, but for now, the women were preparing themselves, organizing, finding their voice, claiming space. The breaking point would come when Amansankrom could no longer bear the burden of corruption and injustice; then would rise the women—not to support changes begun by others, but to lead the change themselves.

It was getting dark by this time; the noises of the day gave way to the muted noises of the night. Nana Adwoa sat in her compound with her daughter, her work finally done, and the evening quiet around her. The food was prepared for her family, and the countless tasks that began before sunrise and stretched far into the day were at last complete.

"You are tired, Mama," Akua Safoa said to her, observing the lines of exhaustion etched upon her face.

"Yes," Nana Adwoa replied, "but tomorrow I will rise again, and the day after, and the day after that. This is what we do, Akua. We endure. We persist. We maintain. Not because we are weak but because we are strong. Not because we accept things as they are but because we are building toward things as they should be."

The struggle was far from over; indeed, in many ways, it was only just beginning, but the women of Amansankrom were ready for whatever was to come. In many ways, they had been preparing for generations, even if they didn't always know what they were preparing for.

Now, as the crisis approached, their preparation was to be tested, their strength revealed, to the community, to themselves, and to the chief who had so long underestimated them.

Chapter 6: Tribulations and Everyday Interplays

The promise of a new day in Amansankrom was often heralded by the smell of woodsmoke and the distant, rhythmic twa-twa-twa of cocoa being split open in the fields. But the morning following the quiet, determined resolve of Nana Adwoa and Akua Safoa, the peace was shattered not by the mundane rhythm of toil, but by a sound far more corrosive to the soul of the community: the ragged, broken wail of a woman whose patience had finally been exhausted.

This was the sound of the trial beginning. The struggle that had been brewing in the quiet of litigation papers and the hushed conversations of women had, by the dawn's early light, become a visible, physical invasion of the village's sanctity.

The wailing belonged to Mama Serwah, a woman whose life was a silent testament to endurance. For thirty years, she had survived on a modest, sloping plot of cocoa farm inherited from her husband, its yield enough to feed her three grandchildren and pay the modest school fees. Mama Serwah was the living embodiment of the 'Everyday Interplays' that sustained Amansankrom; she was the small, fragile thread of stability that Kwaku Bonsam had now decided to cut.

She stood at the corner of the market square, where the main street turned towards the royal palace, pointing a trembling finger at two men who moved with the officious, heavy-handed authority of borrowed power. One was the Chief's new court clerk, a greasy, young man from Kumasi whose spectacles sat perpetually askew, giving him an air of confused superiority. The other was a man of the town, Kojo Nsiah, known for his debt and his recent, sudden friendship with the Chief's inner circle—a friendship that granted him a cruel, petty license he had never earned.

The clerk carried a scroll, rolled tight like a whip, and Nsiah carried a length of brightly colored tape—ribbons of red and white, gaudy symbols of dispossession. They were marking off Mama Serwah's cocoa plot, the small farm she had already begun to clear for the season.

"It is signed by the District Commissioner!" the clerk shouted over Serwah's cries, tapping the scroll impatiently. "It is legally transacted! The land is now the property of His Worship, the Chief, and will be used for the development of the community!"

This lie—the cloak of 'community development'—was the chosen garment for every act of naked thievery Kwaku Bonsam committed. The land was not destined for a hospital or a school; it was destined for resale to a timber consortium that would strip the hillside bare, leaving erosion and silence in its wake.

The crowd gathered quickly, drawn by the sound of distress and the spectacle of the red and white tape. They watched, tight-lipped and immobile, trapped in the moral paralysis that had afflicted Amansankrom since Kwaku Bonsam's contested enstoolment. Each person knew the injustice was profound, but each also measured the distance between their own modest holdings and the Chief's long reach. To speak was to risk their own fields, their own children's future.

But it was precisely this moment that Nana Adwoa had anticipated. Her conversation with Akua Safoa the previous night had been the final seal of the contract the women had formed: that they would not endure the breaking of their sisters. They would not wait for the men who were bound by litigation and history to act.

Nana Adwoa emerged from her compound with a stride that, though not swift, was filled with a deliberate, spiritual weight. She was joined immediately by Akua Safoa and three other senior market women, all dressed in their dark, solid wrappers, signifying their age and unwavering position in the community. Their entry into the square was not a rush, but a measured advance—a slow-moving tide of feminine authority that parted the paralyzed crowd.

Nana Adwoa did not address the clerk or the Chief's man. She walked straight to Mama Serwah, wrapped a calming arm around the distraught woman, and spoke in a low, clear voice that cut through the clerk's blustering.

"The spirit of the land is not in your deed, Mama," she said. "It is in your sweat. It is in the feet of your children who have walked its rows."

Then, turning to face the clerk, her gaze was not one of supplication, but of ancient judgment.

"The deed you carry is a piece of paper dyed with the ink of corruption," Nana Adwoa stated, her voice now resonant, carrying across the square. "But the law of Amansankrom is written upon the earth itself, witnessed by the ancestors and upheld by the living. This woman has tended this land by the grace of God and the spirit of her forebears. By what ancestral law does your master, the Chief, claim it now?"

The clerk, flustered by this direct appeal to traditional authority—an authority he understood only in terms of bribes, not spiritual duty—fumbled with his spectacles. "It is State law, madam! The Chief has a judicial ruling! You are interfering with the process!"

"There is no State law that supersedes the law of justice in a good man's heart," Nana Adwoa countered. "And there is no judicial ruling that can steal a widow's last sustenance without the earth itself crying out against the thief. If this man's seizure is just, let him come and face the community that fed his father, and explain how he justifies the starvation of his mother."

Kojo Nsiah, the town's own collaborator, found his courage draining away under the combined, silent stare of the women. He hesitated with the red tape. He had expected fear, not this calm, collective condemnation.

The stalemate held for a dangerous, suspended moment, until the air thickened with the approach of the inevitable. A sleek, black Land Cruiser—a recent, garish acquisition that stood in sharp contrast to the dusty simplicity of the village— rolled into the square and braked sharply. Out stepped Chief Kwaku Bonsam, magnificent and terrible in a black and gold kente cloth, his face set in an expression of imperial displeasure.

He did not walk; he descended upon the scene, his heavy, golden sandals striking the earth like hammers. The gathered crowd instinctively retreated, their hands shielding their mouths in a traditional gesture of respect mixed with terror. Even Nana Adwoa's group tensed, but did not move.

"What is this spectacle?" Kwaku Bonsam roared, addressing the crowd but looking straight at Nana Adwoa. "A simple legal matter, and the old dogs of this town howl like hungry jackals! You," he leveled a finger at Nana Adwoa, his eyes narrowing to slits. "You lead this resistance. You teach insubordination. You forget that the stool you respect is my seat, and my word is the final law!"

Nana Adwoa met his gaze, unflinching. The strength of her conviction—the cumulative preparation of generations—was now her armor.

"Nana Chief," she began, using the title with a deliberate inflection that acknowledged the office, but not the man. "We do not howl. We speak. And we speak for the truth that you have wrapped in lies. The land of Mama Serwah is ancestral ground. You use a foreign legal document to undo a sacred covenant. You have stolen the past, and you are starving the future."

Kwaku Bonsam gave a short, hard laugh that held no humor. "A sacred covenant? A starving future? These are the myths of old women, Nana Adwoa. I speak the language of progress and development! The town will prosper, but not by clinging to the dusty farms of widows! This town needs capital, investment, and a Chief who understands how the new world operates. You cling to the fetish of tradition, but tradition cannot pay for electricity!"

"If a thousand years of tradition has taught us to protect the least among us, and the new world teaches you to rob a grieving woman," Nana Adwoa retorted, her voice rising slightly, "then the new world has nothing to teach us but shame. If you proceed with this seizure, you are not a chief, but a thief on a gilded stool. And the stool will shake under you."

The silence that followed was heavy, pregnant with historical significance. No one—not the elders, not the men entangled in his litigation—had dared to speak such words to Kwaku Bonsam since his ascension. The Chief, enraged by the public defiance, stepped closer, his face a mask of fury.

"You threaten me, old woman?" he hissed, dropping the formal address. "The stool does not shake. I will remove the tongue of anyone who dares to challenge my authority. Let this be clear to all of Amansankrom: Mama Serwah's land is forfeit. It is a legal fact. If I see a single soul set foot upon that land, they will not merely be fined. They will be removed from this community entirely. Go home. Prepare your food. Tend your children. I am your leader, and my patience is ended."

He signaled his guards, who, empowered by his rage, roughly pushed the crowd back. The clerk, heartened, quickly finished marking the final perimeter of the stolen land.

Kwaku Bonsam stood for another long moment, his chest heaving, ensuring the weight of his threat settled into the bones of every witness. Then, he turned and got back into the black

Land Cruiser, which sped away in a cloud of dust—a mechanical, modern symbol of his brutal, unyielding power.

Nana Adwoa did not move until the vehicle was out of sight. She then helped Mama Serwah, now utterly broken, away from the scene. The battle for the land was lost, but the battle for the soul of the community—the 'Tribulation' itself—had officially begun. For the first time, Kwaku Bonsam knew what he faced: not a group of disgruntled men arguing over protocol, but a force of women who understood that injustice, if left unchallenged, would consume the entire village.

The cost of this first, direct confrontation was yet to be tallied, but the air in Amansankrom had changed. The town was now divided, standing at the precipice of civil war, a perfect, tense atmosphere for the power struggles and rivalries that must now emerge from the shadows.

The cloud of dust raised by the Chief's hasty departure settled slowly, coating the market square in a fine, ochre silt that felt like a burial shroud over the morning's failed defense. The crowd, which had witnessed the unprecedented defiance of Nana Adwoa and the immediate, brutal counter-stroke of Kwaku Bonsam, did not cheer or cry out in communal solidarity. Instead, they dissolved. They melted away into the surrounding side streets, carrying the unbearable weight of the confrontation back to their homes, their shops, and their farms. The true test of Nana Adwoa's action was not in the moment of confrontation, but in the hours that followed, as the witnesses wrestled with the choice they had been forced to recognize: resistance or compliance.

The battle for the land was over, but the war for the loyalty of the townspeople had just begun.

The immediate locus of this internal struggle coalesced around the small palm wine shed of Maame Esi, a place where, traditionally, men would discuss matters of land, harvest, and the community's political health. Today, however, the discussions were sharp, fractured, and laced with a fear that spoiled the taste of the fresh sap.

Kojo Nsiah, the collaborator who had earlier held the ribbon of dispossession, was now aggressively drinking, attempting to restore the courage that had momentarily failed him under Nana Adwoa's gaze. He was surrounded by a handful of other men—minor shopkeepers and debtors whose precarious financial status bound them to the Chief's camp like hostages. Nsiah, having been publicly shamed, now sought public vindication.

"The Chief spoke the truth!" Nsiah spat, slamming his cup down onto the rough wooden table. "These women—they are reckless. They speak of tradition, but they dishonor the Stool by speaking disrespectfully to its occupant! Who are they to dictate law? Are they lawyers? Are they elders? They are market women!"

Opanyin Kofi Twum, a respected but cautious elder whose family ties were strong but whose business interests lay outside of the Chief's immediate land schemes, raised a hand, attempting to inject a measure of ancient wisdom into the rising heat.

"Kojo, we must respect the ancient order," Opanyin Twum began, his voice weary. "The stool is sacred. But the Chief's behavior… seizing a widow's farm under false pretext… this is a violation of the sacred trust. The Stool demands protection of the vulnerable, not their exploitation."

"The Stool demands obedience!" Nsiah countered, leaning in, his breath heavy with palm wine. "And progress! You cling to dusty tradition, Opanyin, while the Chief is securing investment from Accra—timber deals, mining licenses! He brings roads and electricity, not your grandmother's superstitions! Nana Adwoa is obstructing progress! She is inviting the government to intervene and dissolve the chieftaincy altogether because of her foolish pride!"

This was the core of Kwaku Bonsam's propaganda: framing his corruption as a modern necessity and the defense of ancestral rights as an obstructive reaction. It was a powerful argument, because many younger men and those with external business contacts genuinely believed that the Chief, however flawed, was the only one who could navigate the complexities of the modern Ghanaian state. Nana Adwoa, in this narrative, was not a revolutionary but an antique, threatening their ability to join the global marketplace.

"She is protecting the very ground we stand on," Twum insisted, rubbing the smooth wood of the table. "Without the land, where is the progress? The town is not a corporation, Kojo. It is a living, spiritual entity. When the living steal from the ancestors, the town dies."

"The town will only die when the men stand by and let the women invite the wrath of the Chief!" Nsiah retorted, his voice rising to a dangerous pitch. "He said it himself: there will be consequences. Fines! Exile! We now have stability—even if it is expensive. Nana Adwoa is bringing chaos! We must silence this dissent before it brings ruin to all of us!"

The sentiment was repeated in the quieter confines of the elder's compounds. Old men, bound by the rigid etiquette of the Stool, spoke in hushed tones, torn between their moral disapproval of Kwaku Bonsam and their deep-seated patriarchal anxiety regarding Nana Adwoa's usurpation of political agency.

Opanyin Kwabena Manu, the oldest and most respected of the neutral elders, sat in his cool, dark compound, receiving various visitors. Opanyin Manu had been the most vocal critic of the Chief's enthronement, yet he had remained aloof from the women's direct actions. He believed that corruption must be fought, but only through the prescribed legal and traditional channels—channels that Kwaku Bonsam had long since co-opted or rendered ineffective.

"It was reckless, Nana Adwoa's action," Opanyin Manu whispered to the man beside him, a schoolteacher named Mr. Appiah, who had witnessed the scene. "Bold, yes. Righteous, yes. But reckless. When a woman stands before the Chief in the open square and accuses him of theft, she does not just endanger herself. She endangers the entire legal foundation of our resistance."

Mr. Appiah, a man whose modern education clashed fiercely with his reverence for tradition, nodded slowly. "But Opanyin, the legal foundation has been eroded by the Chief's bribing of the judges and his control of the records. It is a foundation made of sand! When the legal structures fail, what then remains but the moral authority of the people? And today, only Nana Adwoa spoke with that authority."

Manu sighed, the sound a rasp in his throat, a sound of history's heavy burden. "The Chief will not see morality, only insubordination. He will not see justice; he will only see a challenge to his power. Her action was public, immediate, and utterly unprecedented. It places every family at risk. We, the elders, have been fighting him in court, using the rules. She has thrown the rules away! The Chief's loyalists will now use this to accuse us all of supporting the dissolution of the Stool. We are now divided, forced to choose between the women's righteous chaos and the men's expensive stability."

The real tragedy of the internal rivalry was that the males, who were preoccupied with the mode of resistance (procedure, litigation), perceived the women's activity as a betrayal of their strategy rather than as a necessary development of the conflict. The women perceived the men's constant legal wrangling as moral cowardice since they were more concerned with the content of resistance (justice, protection of the weak).

The lines of rivalry were not merely drawn between the Chief's men and the townspeople; they were drawn between the Legalists (men) and the Moralists (women), between Compliance (Kojo Nsiah) and Conscience (Nana Adwoa).

As the town dissolved into these fearful, internal debates, Nana Adwoa and Akua Safoa retreated to the Queen Mother's compound, the traditional heart of feminine power in Amansankrom. Here, protected from the immediate clamor, they gathered the core group of market women who had been instrumental in their secret organizational work. The meeting was not for mourning the loss of Mama Serwah's land—that was a strategic casualty they had prepared for—but for anticipating the backlash.

Nana Adwoa stood before the women, her posture conveying the same unyielding dignity she had shown the Chief.

"The trial has begun," she declared, bypassing all greetings. "We have sacrificed Mama Serwah's land to the Chief's anger, but we have won the attention of the town. Before today, the Chief's corruption was a thick blanket of fear. Now, there is a hole in that blanket, and the light of truth has shone through. The town has seen that Kwaku Bonsam is a thief, and that the women dare to call him one."

Akua Safoa, ever the pragmatist, spoke next, addressing the practicalities of the brewing rivalry. "The men are speaking against us. They accuse us of being careless. They claim that the Chief will now take revenge on our families because we have jeopardized the lawsuit. By accusing us of being agents of chaos and subverting the established order, Kojo Nsiah is blatantly contradicting himself."

A younger woman, Afia, whose husband was already facing a minor, manufactured lawsuit over a tax dispute, spoke up, her voice trembling slightly. "My husband says I must cease meeting with you, Nana Adwoa. He says the Chief will know. The fear is spreading faster than the news."

Nana Adwoa's expression softened a little when she recognized the tremendous strain the men were now placing on their wives. The Chief's most successful tactic was to create dissension within the family.

"Tell your husband, Afia, that the greatest danger is not in fighting the Chief, but in living under him," Nana Adwoa advised gently. "We did not act to destroy the law; we acted because the Chief has already destroyed it. Our fight is not just for the land, but for the moral soul of the town. When the men are afraid to speak, it is the duty of the mothers to speak for their children."

The group dispersed, not out of dread, but with a new, quiet confidence. They had publicly declared their opposition to the Chief; however, the more significant conflict was now internal: they were striving to win the affection of their spouses, fathers, and neighbors before Kwaku Bonsam's system of fear and bribery became an unchallenged, absolute authority. The town of Amansankrom was no longer a cohesive entity; it was a collection of shattered loyalties, trembling in the presence of the two colossal forces of a perfidious Chief and a defiant woman.

The women's silent retreat from the market square was an act of strategic calculation. They had delivered their message to the Chief, and now they had to manage the consequences of that declaration. The true nature of Kwaku Bonsam's retaliation unfolded not in loud confrontations or legal filings, but in the slow, meticulous strangulation of the community's economic life—the ultimate impact of corruption on daily life.

The immediate effect of the punitive market taxes was a chilling and tangible hunger. For the poorest segments of Amansankrom, the 20 percent increase in staples like smoked fish and dried cassava resulted in an instantaneous reduction in nutritional intake. This was not a slow famine, but a sudden, tactical deprivation engineered to break the spirit of the resistance before it could fully coalesce.

The sight of children, their usual boisterous energy subdued, standing near the stalls with empty bowls, became the most painful testament to the Chief's malice. These were the innocents, the very future Nana Adwoa and the women sought to protect, now serving as unintended casualties in the political war. The women, who had organized themselves with such foresight, were now forced to activate their Mutual Aid Cooperative—the secret mechanism of solidarity they had established to circumvent just such a crisis.

After a tiring day at the market and a fight with her husband, Kobina, Akua Safoa spent the evening pacing the back alleyways of the hamlet. She discreetly carried a basket covered with a plain cloth that contained bags of dry beans and reserved gari (cassava meal) instead of her typical trade products. The old, the ill, and the families whose primary breadwinners were absent or dealing with the Chief's fabricated litigation were the only people she stopped at, moving like a shadow.

This covert distribution was fraught with danger. If Kwaku Bonsam's loyalists—or worse, his new revenue agents—

discovered the women were actively circumventing his economic blockade, the punishment would be swift and far more severe than a simple fine. They would be accused of economic sabotage, an offense the Chief could easily redefine as treason against the Stool.

At the compound of Mama Serwah, the widow whose land seizure had triggered the conflict, Akua paused. Mama Serwah sat in the dark, her grief not expressed in tears, but in a profound, internal silence. She was now economically destitute, relying entirely on the fragile network of community support.

"The salmon is here, Mama," Akua whispered, placing the basket gently on the ground. "And enough gari for the week. You will not starve. Nana Adwoa sends her love and her assurance that the earth will remember the thief who stole it from a widow."

Mama Serwah nodded, her eyes closed, accepting the assistance with the dignity of one who recognizes that they are being sustained by a moral covenant that is more powerful than any legal document. "Tell Nana Adwoa that the earth remembers everything, my daughter. It is slow to move, but it is absolute in its judgment."

The profound sense of displacement and insecurity extended far beyond the realm of commerce. The chieftaincy dispute, once confined to the legal documents of Accra, had now invaded the sanctity of the household, manifesting as crippling marital discord and patriarchal pressure.

The men of Amansankrom—the fathers, the husbands, the brothers—now faced an unbearable choice. They could support the women, their conscience aligning with the justice represented by Nana Adwoa, but risk the economic ruin of their families. Or they could enforce their household authority, commanding their wives and sisters to cease their organizational activities, thereby buying a fragile, temporary peace from the Chief.

The pressure exerted by the Chief's loyalists, particularly Kojo Nsiah and the more fearful elders, found its primary expression in the domestic sphere. Husbands began to forbid their wives from attending the women's quiet, essential gatherings. They argued with a desperate logic: The Chief will only punish those who draw attention to themselves. We must be invisible to survive.

This was a direct, calculated attack on the very cohesion of the resistance. Kwaku Bonsam, by striking at the market and turning husbands against wives, sought to destroy the women's power by dissolving their organization at its domestic base. The women of Amansankrom now had two fronts to fight: the visible tyranny of the Chief outside, and the invisible tyranny of fear inside their own walls.

Akua Safoa's return to her compound that night was met with the cold, thick silence of her husband, Kobina. He was not angry in the customary sense; rather, he was enveloped by a powerful, crippling fear that made him withdrawn and authoritarian.

He had heard the discussions in the palm-wine shed, where men like Kojo Nsiah, acting as the Chief's unwitting mouthpieces, had accused Akua's mother and her co-conspirators of being agents of societal breakdown. Kobina saw the Chief's retribution not as a test of courage, but as a test of marital compliance.

"Where have you been, Akua?" Kobina asked, his voice low, lacking its usual warmth.

"I was securing the necessary credit for the market tomorrow, Kobina," she lied smoothly, unwilling to endanger him with the truth of the Mutual Aid deliveries.

"Your mother's credit, Akua," he corrected, his eyes fixed on her. "The credit that will lead the Chief to our door. The timber delivery for the school construction was stopped today. Tanko told the driver the paperwork was 'incomplete.' It is a direct warning to me, Akua. They know you are her daughter. They know you are active."

He stood up, planting himself between her and the door. The familiar structure of their marriage was dissolving under the weight of this external pressure, transforming partnership into command.

"I have forbidden you to continue your work with the market council," he stated, his voice trembling slightly—a tremor that spoke more of panic than resolution. "We are a family, Akua. I must protect us. Until this foolishness ends, you will tend to the house and the children, and you will stay away from the women's meetings."

Akua Safoa looked at her husband, seeing not the Chief's brutality, but the terrifying vulnerability of the average man who valued stability over justice. His command was a desperate attempt to regain control in a world where the Chief had taken everything else.

"Kobina, I will never choose the money that feeds us over the morality that sustains us," Akua replied, her voice steady and profoundly sad. "The Chief has already determined our fate. Your obedience will not save your business; it will only delay the inevitable and rob you of your dignity. When I fight to feed the starving, I fight for your own soul."

Her statements impacted him, causing him to make a noticeable flinch. However, the fear of economic devastation, the fear of Tanko's cudgel, and Kwaku Bonsam's Land Cruiser was a more urgent and overwhelming force than the concept of moral dignity, which was more of an abstract concept. The man's realistic fear and the woman's radical hope were pitted against one another in their family, which had become a battleground for ideas, just like the entire town's household had become. Kobina walked away, unable to enforce his command, yet unable to yield to her truth. The marital discord hung in the air like smoke, a heavy, invisible impact of the corruption.

Nana Adwoa, resting in her own compound, understood this painful reality. The resistance had to be subtle, self-sustaining, and emotionally resilient enough to withstand not only the Chief's economic sanctions but the internal fracturing of the households. The women had endured generations of marginalization; they had developed the necessary psychological fortitude to withstand this new, targeted pressure. Their greatest strength was their quiet understanding that the Everyday Interplays, the feeding of the family, the tending of the market, were not chores, but acts of profound, political resistance.

The Tribulations were now fully engaged. The town was hungry, divided, and afraid. But the fire of defiance, though dampened by fear, was not extinguished. It burned low and steady in the compounds, ready to rise again in the next stage of the struggle. This entire dilemma did not close with a clear victory, but with the weary, profound understanding that true resistance begins when the cost of inaction becomes higher than the cost of action.

The women were committed to paying that price.

Chapter 7: Heritage and History

The true struggle in Amansankrom, Nana Adwoa understood, was not for land or money, but for the moral lexicon of the town. Kwaku Bonsam had seized the narrative, convincing many that their hardships were merely the necessary price of 'progress' and that resistance was a futile attachment to a dusty, irrelevant past.

After the public setback in the market, where the women's courage had been met with crippling taxes and domestic division, a direct, visible challenge was impossible; the war had to retreat from the physical square into the intellectual landscape of the community.

The chosen battlefield was memory, and the strategy was an ancient one: the philosophy of Sankofa.

The word "Sankofa," which conjures up a powerful image of a bird reaching back to retrieve an egg, was more than just a proverb; it was a fundamental value that the Kwahu people adhered to. The lesson that one must turn to the past in order to comprehend the present and construct the future was taught by it. Nana Adwoa saw it as the ideal intellectual counterpoint to the Chief's reckless modernity, and she believed that it was essential.

She convened the first of the Sankofa Sessions not in the central, obvious locations, but in the quiet, low-roofed assembly room behind the Queen Mother's compound. The attendees were a careful mixture: the unyielding core of market women (Akua Safoa, Afia), a handful of university students who felt politically alienated, and, crucially, a few of the fearful, fence-sitting men who, like Akua's husband, Kobina, were desperate for a way to resist without risking economic annihilation.

It was a deliberate rejection of the Chief's reliance on the unreliable and expensive electricity that he advocated for, and the room was illuminated by a solitary kerosene lamp. The light from the lamp was soft and wavering, and it created lengthy shadows that moved around.

When Nana Adwoa stood before them, she was not dressed in the regalia of a warrior but rather in a plain, dark fabric. Her posture was one of quiet authority that could not be shaken. She did not discuss the market taxes; rather, she discussed the roots of the taxes.

"The Chief, in his frenzy for timber deals and modern deeds, has told you that we are weak because we look back," Nana Adwoa began, her voice low and resonant, cutting through the anxiety in the room. "He claims that to look to the Kwahu origins of Amansankrom is to be backward. I tell you that this claim is a profound lie—a poison he feeds your ears to weaken your hearts."

She detailed the history known by every true Kwahu elder, but now often forgotten by the modern generation: the migrations, the hardships, and the fundamental pact that defined their settlement. They were not people who sought a simple life, but a governed life—a people whose very history was rooted in the careful, ethical organization of the political realm.

"We are not refugees, living by accident," she explained. "We are the people of the mountains, who brought with us the most sacred duty: the duty to protect the moral integrity of the Stool. Our ancestors did not settle here to escape authority; they settled here to establish righteous authority under the true Akan law."

She paused, allowing the weight of this heritage—the understanding that their existence was a testament to an ancient, principled political tradition—to settle.

"The concept of Sankofa," she continued, moving toward a small, carved wooden representation of the bird, "is not about dwelling on the past. It is about retrieving what is essential for survival. What has Kwaku Bonsam stolen from us, beyond the land of Mama Serwah and the money of the market?"

A young student, Emelia, whose father had been pressured into silence, spoke up hesitantly. "He has stolen our dignity, Nana. We cannot look each other in the eye in the market."

"Yes, dignity," Nana Adwoa affirmed. "And what else? He has stolen the very meaning of the title he wears."

This was the core of the ideological assault. Nana Adwoa proceeded to dismantle the Chief's authority by leveraging the very title he demanded: Nana.

"Kwaku Bonsam forces you to call him Nana," she said. "He believes this title is a symbol of absolute power, like a king's crown. But what does Nana truly mean in our Kwahu tongue? It is a term of profound respect for an elder, a recognition of wisdom, justice, and the embodiment of the ancestral covenant."

She looked directly at the men in the room, particularly Kobina, who sat rigid against the back wall.

"A true Nana does not use the law of the state to rob a widow. A true Nana does not turn a father against his son, nor a husband against his wife. A true Nana is the spiritual guarantor of the community's well-being. Kwaku Bonsam, by his actions, has become the moral and spiritual antithesis of what the title demands. He is not a guardian; he is a predator. Therefore, when you call him Nana, you are forced to tell a lie."

This reinterpretation was groundbreaking. It provided a means of escape for the men, who were compelled by culture to honor the title. They were honoring the greater, authentic meaning of the Nana title, which the Chief himself had soiled, rather than showing contempt for their leader.

Nana Adwoa was ruling by definition; the Chief had done it by intimidation.

"We must use Sankofa to retrieve the true definition," she emphasized. "We look to the past to find the uncorrupted moral law that Kwaku Bonsam has polluted. This law is simple: The Stool serves the people; the Chief is the Stool's servant. Kwaku Bonsam has reversed this; he demands that the people serve him."

The discussion then shifted to the potential for political mobilization that this ideological shift would enable. Akua

Safoa, recovering her political voice after the anxiety of the domestic conflict, spoke next, addressing the fearful men.

"We saw the market today," Akua said, her voice sharp with the memory of the theft. "The Chief's greed is endless. Your obedience, Kobina, will only encourage him to ask for more. He will eventually take your timber contract, regardless of how quiet I am. You cannot appease a hungry spirit by giving it a small offering; you must starve the spirit itself."

She presented the new strategy, derived entirely from the Sankofa philosophy: "We will no longer waste our energy fighting the new taxes—that is his battlefield. We will use the history that Nana Adwoa teaches us to prove that the Chief is illegitimate according to our own ancestral laws. We will document every violation—not the tax rates, but the spiritual crimes: the desecration of the Stool's oath, the betrayal of the land covenant, and the failure to honor the Akwasidae observances."

The guys were finally given a directive for action that was culturally acceptable, and Kobina's slow and deliberate nod served as the driver of this directive. The people were not rebelling against the state; rather, they were safeguarding the cultural heritage that they considered to be sacrosanct.

"We are shifting the battle from the court of Accra, which is corrupted by his money, to the court of our Ancestors, which is governed by truth," Nana Adwoa concluded. "This is the wisdom of Sankofa. We must look back to retrieve the moral authority that the present has stolen. In the next days, we will document where the Chief has failed this oath. We will visit the sacred places, the landmarks he has profaned, and we will gather the evidence of his spiritual illegitimacy. Our strength is not in our fists or our purses, but in the uncorrupted history of the Kwahu people."

The session broke up quietly. The attendees did not leave with shouts of revolutionary zeal, but with a firm, sober sense of duty. The women had successfully transformed themselves from market protestors into cultural custodians. The men, though still wary, had been given a powerful new vocabulary to resist the Chief's tyranny without feeling like traitors to their own traditional political structure. The battle for the heart of Amansankrom had been won; now, they had to prove it with evidence. The next step was to venture out and collect the physical evidence of the Chief's spiritual crimes.

The Sacred Geography of Resistance

The strategic task emanating from the Sankofa Sessions was not to argue with the Chief's men, but to document the incontrovertible evidence of his spiritual illegitimacy. Kwaku Bonsam had been successful in corrupting paper laws; he had not yet learned that the laws of the earth and the laws of the ancestors resisted bribery. Nana Adwoa directed her daughter, Akua Safoa, and two trusted, younger women, Emelia and Afia, to undertake this critical reconnaissance. Their mission was to visit the historically significant sites of Amansankrom— the landmarks that embodied the town's true, unwritten constitution.

The Chief's power was centered in the new administrative block and the market. The women's power lay in the forgotten, sacred geography of the periphery.

Their first target was the Akwasidae Grove, a small, carefully maintained clearing near the oldest silk-cotton tree, slightly removed from the main town center. This grove was traditionally used for the Akwasidae festival, the revered bi-weekly observance where the Chief, acting as the spiritual intermediary, poured libations to honour the ancestors and reaffirm the sacred oath of the Stool. It was a place of profound purity, where the boundary between the living and the dead was thinnest.

Kwahu tradition said that the grove had to be carefully taken care of. It had to be swept every day, kept clean of modern trash, and only allowed to be used for sacred reasons. It had been known for years that the Chief didn't follow the Akwasidae rules, but the state of the wood would show how seriously he broke the rules.

Akua Safoa, leading the small party, moved with the quiet stealth of a hunter. The journey was short but marked by a growing sense of dread. As they approached the familiar, high canopy of the silk-cotton tree, the expected atmosphere of stillness and reverence was violently absent. Instead of the quiet humidity and the earthy smell of reverence, the air was thick with the scent of stagnant water and refuse.

They emerged into the clearing, and the sight was a violent affront to their heritage.

The Akwasidae Grove had not merely been neglected; it had been actively defiled. Where the ancestral shrine—a small, carefully smoothed granite boulder—once sat upon clean earth, it was now obscured by a scattering of modern waste. Empty plastic water sachets, discarded metal shards from construction (likely from the Chief's new development projects), and—most galling of all—the broken remains of cheap, imported liquor bottles lay scattered across the hallowed ground.

The visual impact was profound, instantly confirming Nana Adwoa's ideological assessment. Kwaku Bonsam, a man obsessed with modern consumption and quick profits, had treated the very spiritual heart of Amansankrom as a mere refuse dump for the detritus of his development schemes.

"This is... this is wicked, Akua. He has turned the ancestors' meeting place into a public latrine." Emelia, the youngest, gasped, covering her mouth with her hand.

Akua Safoa felt a deep, cold certainty settle in her heart. This was more powerful than any bribed land deed. This was an irrefutable spiritual crime. Kwaku Bonsam's failure to honour the sacred site meant that his very existence as Nana— a title demanding Respect for Elders and the maintenance of the traditional covenant—was a sham.

She knelt, carefully picking up a shard of bright green glass, examining it with meticulous care. "We must document this. Every piece of refuse, every overturned stone. We are not just recording trash; we are recording the Chief's moral confession."

They spent the next hour working with painful reverence, meticulously cataloging the defilement. Akua sketched the layout of the grove in a small notebook, noting the proximity of the trash to the ancestral stone. The younger women, Emelia and Afia, counted and categorized the specific items of waste, noting the brands of cheap beer and the types of construction materials, linking the spiritual defilement directly to the Chief's corrupt business ventures.

The Ancient Stool House

Their second destination was the Ancient Stool House, a small, unassuming structure tucked away near the old market which housed the non-sacred regalia and records. This site was significant because it represented the physical continuity of traditional leadership. The Chief rarely visited it, preferring the grand, modern, concrete palace he had built closer to the main road.

The Stool House was guarded not by the Chief's expensive security, but by a single, frail, elderly man named Opanyin Yaw, a traditionalist who had refused the Chief's bribes. Yaw had served the Stool since childhood, and his loyalty was to the institution, not the occupant.

Opanyin Yaw received the women with a weary, knowing look, recognizing them instantly as Nana Adwoa's envoys. "You have come to see what the modern tongue calls 'evidence,' haven't you?" he whispered, his voice dry as parchment.

Akua Safoa nodded respectfully. "We have come to see the truth, Opanyin."

He ushered them into the dark, dusty interior. The air inside was heavy with the scent of aged wood and history. He pointed to a high shelf where the true, ancient Black Stool was traditionally kept, now sadly empty—Kwaku Bonsam had controversially moved it to his palace, claiming it needed 'modern security,' a move many traditionalists considered a spiritual theft.

Opanyin Yaw then led them to a large, teak cabinet where the traditional clothing, including the revered Kente cloth, was meant to be stored.

"Look inside," he commanded.

Akua Safoa opened the cabinet. Inside, the venerable cloths were stuffed carelessly, stained not with age but with what appeared to be engine grease and dampness. They were mixed haphazardly with modern, imported synthetic fabrics—cheap, bright scarves purchased for some recent, low-grade political rally. The sacred symbols woven into the Kente—which spoke volumes about the Kwahu origins and the Chief's oath—were treated with the disregard of dirty rags.

Opanyin Yaw struck the cabinet with the back of his hand, producing a dull, resonant thud. "The true crime, Nana Adwoa's daughter, is not that he steals the money. It is that he does not care for the things that define us. He wears the Kente when the photographers are here, but he leaves it here to rot when the camera is gone. He treats our heritage like a costume, not a covenant."

He then revealed the final, devastating piece of evidence: the traditional Record Ledger of the Stool House. This book contained the documented lineages, the oaths of previous chiefs, and, crucially, the original land covenants drawn not on government forms, but in the elaborate, metaphorical language of the Kwahu people.

"The Chief sent his agent for this book last month," Opanyin Yaw whispered, clutching the heavy volume. "He wanted to 'modernize the records.' But I refused. He tried to bribe me with money to buy my silence, but my silence is not for sale."

In spite of her weariness, Akua Safoa bowed down and painstakingly traced the ancient script on the ledger's cover. The Chief's obsession with eradicating or altering this book proved beyond a reasonable doubt that the spiritual law was his sole safeguard against total dominion.

The Weapon of Evidence

The return journey to Nana Adwoa's compound was conducted in weighted silence. The women did not need to speak; the physical evidence of the defilement spoke louder than any sermon. They had found their weapon: not a philosophical argument, but the grotesque, documented reality of the Chief's spiritual neglect.

The Sankofa philosophy was now fully vindicated. By looking to the past (the sacred Grove, the Stool House), they had retrieved the essential truth stolen by the present (the Chief's corruption). That night, Akua Safoa presented her sketches, her notes on the refuse, and her testimony regarding the ruined Kente to her mother. Nana Adwoa listened, her expression darkening with each detail.

"He has signed his own warrant, Akua," Nana Adwoa said finally, her voice low but firm. "The Regional House of Chiefs may ignore a financial dispute, but they cannot ignore the profanation of the Akwasidae Grove or the desecration of the sacred regalia. This is an offense against the ancestors, against our very history. We have the evidence. Now, we must use it to bring the Legalists—the men who fear the Chief's money—into our fold."

The Statement of Heritage

The photographs and sketches of the defiled Akwasidae Grove, along with Opanyin Yaw's testimony regarding the abandoned Stool regalia, represented the culmination of the women's new strategic pivot. Kwaku Bonsam's downfall would not be engineered through a financial audit or a modern court ruling, both of which his corruption could easily bypass. His vulnerability lay in the spiritual compact that was the foundation of the chieftaincy itself. His power could only be dismantled by proving his betrayal of the Kwahu traditional leadership covenant.

It was up to Nana Adwoa's collective knowledge and the few surviving elders who were both literate and morally upright to turn these heinous spiritual crimes into a formal, legal document that could be used as a weapon in the local seats of power. Chief among these allies was Opanyin Kwabena Manu, a retired schoolteacher who had previously been too cautious to support the women's public activism, but who now saw the irrefutable evidence of the Chief's sacrilege. Manu's fear of state retaliation was finally surpassed by his profound fear of ancestral condemnation.

Opanyin Manu sat hunched over a heavy, pristine sheet of parchment in the Queen Mother's inner courtyard. The afternoon sun cast a warm, solemn light on the ink as he composed the Statement of Heritage. This was not a complaint about stolen money; it was a theological indictment. The document meticulously detailed three principal charges, framing them as threats to the stability and spiritual health of the entire Kwahu region:

1. **The Violation of the Akwasidae Covenant:** Nana Adwoa dictated the specifics: the Chief's systematic neglect of the bi-weekly Akwasidae rites, the failure to honor the ancestors, and the grotesque profanation of the sacred grove by allowing it to become a dumping ground for the waste of his private construction projects. This charge was the heaviest; it proved the Chief had willingly and consciously severed the essential link between the living community and the honored dead, leaving the town dangerously exposed to spiritual misfortune.

2. **The Profanation of Traditional Regalia and Records:** It cited the wilful decay of the sacred Kente cloth and ceremonial attire, which embodied the Kwahu origins of their people, and the Chief's attempt to seize and 'modernize' the ancient Stool Ledger. This was proof that the Chief viewed the ancient symbols of office not as powerful, living covenants, but as mere disposable costumes for public display.

3.   The Breach of the Land Covenant: It argued that by seizing Mama Serwah's land for a foreign enterprise—a transaction based purely on modern, personal greed—the Chief had betrayed the fundamental, unwritten law that land belongs to the lineage, not the individual, and that the Stool is merely the custodian, not the owner.

The Statement of Heritage concluded with an appeal to the Regional House of Chiefs. It did not request the immediate destooling of Kwaku Bonsam, which would have sounded like a personal vendetta. Instead, it implored the Regional House to fulfill its duty to preserve cultural heritage by intervening to prevent the Chief's actions from inviting catastrophic ancestral wrath upon the whole region. It was a document designed to trigger the conscience of the traditional establishment, where spiritual law held greater weight than government forms.

The Signatures of Conscience

With the text finalized, the immense challenge of gathering the necessary signatures remained. This final stage of the ideological war required the fearful, pragmatic men—the Legalists—to transition from a tacit agreement to a public, documented commitment.

Akua Safoa, exhausted yet resolute, undertook the task of securing the most critical signature: that of her husband, Kobina. The financial pressure on him was relentless; the Chief's informal blockade on his timber exports had deepened his debt, leaving him hollowed out by anxiety.

She found him sitting alone in the darkened sitting room of their home, the glow of a single battery lantern illuminating his weary face. She did not raise her voice, nor did she resort to the emotional arguments that had failed in the wake of the market confrontation. She placed the Statement before him, open to the signature page.

"Look at the names already here, Kobina," she said, her voice a low, steady current of truth. "Opanyin Manu has signed. The linguist's family has signed. They are men who understand the price of silence is higher than the price of resistance."

Kobina stared at the empty space reserved for his name. He was caught in a brutal, internal crossfire. His practical mind was consumed by the image of his assets—the lorry, the machinery, the timber yard—all dissolving under the Chief's merciless pressure. His cultural soul, however, was haunted by the image of the desecrated Akwasidae Grove, a memory that challenged his very identity as a man of Kwahu origins.

"If I sign this, Akua," he finally articulated, his voice thick with suppressed anguish, "Kwaku Bonsam will finish me. He will seize everything. He will use the government papers to destroy our entire life, claiming I am a traitor to the state, not a man protecting tradition."

Akua moved closer, sitting beside him on the worn sofa. She did not touch him, understanding the need for space, but her presence was a dense, palpable force. "He will take those things anyway, Kobina. You know this. Your silence has not bought you peace; it has only marked you as weak. He sees your fear as his permission."

She leaned slightly closer, speaking to his true, deepest fear: the fear of losing honor. "This document is not a confrontation with the state. It is an act of Sankofa, a retrieval of the essential law that protects your family's dignity. You are not signing as a rebel against the Chief. You are signing as a man of Respect for Elders and the ancestor's truth. If you sign, we will face financial hardship, but we will have the armor of righteousness. If you refuse, we will still face ruin, and we will be stripped bare of honor."

The weight of the unwritten law, the necessity of cultural survival over monetary preservation, finally crushed his resistance. Kobina's hand, though shaking from years of labor and recent anxiety, took up the pen. He signed his name, KOBINA OSEI, in a slow, deliberate script that felt less like an endorsement and more like an oath sworn to the soil itself.

The signature of a man who had everything to lose but chose heritage over wealth was the catalyst the movement needed. Word spread quickly through the network of wives and mothers: Kobina Osei had chosen the ancestors over the Chief's money. Emboldened, other fearful, yet principled men—the heads of minor families, the small-scale traders, the last honest cocoa farmers—came forward in the darkness of the evening to add their names. The women recorded each signature with quiet efficiency, ensuring the men retained the sense that this was their official, male-led defense of the tradition.

The completed Statement of Heritage was a formidable document, bound with twine and sealed with red wax bearing the impression of Nana Adwoa's personal ring. It was the definitive counter-narrative to Kwaku Bonsam's tyrannical rule.

The Dispatch

The final act was the Statement's clandestine dispatch. At the deepest point of night, when the town was truly asleep and the Chief's mercenaries were focused on guarding the roads, Nana Adwoa entrusted the sealed document to Afia, one of the young women who had helped survey the grove. Afia, riding pillion on a fast, small motorcycle driven by her brother—a man whose fear had been cured by the sight of Kobina's signature—sped away from Amansankrom. The package was destined not for the public eye, but for the quiet bureaucracy of the Registrar of the Regional House of Chiefs, the only entity capable of formally recognizing spiritual illegitimacy.

The motorcycle's roar sank into the Kwahu night and left a clean silence. Nana Adwoa stood in it, eyes on the road, steady as a witness who has already sworn the oath. The reckoning had ripened past denial.

Overwhelmed by his triumph in the marketplace, the Chief trusted physical power in the same manner that a sleepwalker trusts a staircase. He was sure to stumble. The exact legacy he professed to protect had been fashioned into a weapon by the ladies, and it waited with the unflappable patience of paper. Power rarely relents without new noise, so trials would go on.

The key weapon was already in the bag. Names matched dates, records were in order, and the lineage spoke with a steady voice. No drum or cudgel could stifle the written and confirmed truth that had made its way into the square.

Chapter 8: The Future of Amansankrom

The dispatch of the Statement of Heritage to the Regional House of Chiefs had not brought about the expected cathartic storm. Instead, Amansankrom was gripped by a profound, unnatural silence—a heavy, expectant quiet far more unsettling than the market shouting or the Chief's mercenaries.

It was the silence of a breath held too long, the moment between a lightning flash and the inevitable crack of thunder.

Days turned into a week, marked only by the relentless passage of the sun across the Kwahu sky. Yet, no official response arrived from the Registrar's office, nor did Chief Kwaku Bonsam betray any awareness that the core of his legitimacy—the spiritual compact of the Stool—had been fundamentally challenged.

The Chief moved with the bored arrogance of a man who believed he had already won. His security detail remained visible but relaxed, confident that the small-scale protests had been crushed and the town's spirit broken by economic punitive measures.

Kwaku Bonsam's ignorance of the specific content of the document—that it was an indictment of spiritual sacrilege and not a mere political petition—was the women's greatest asset. He was expecting another argument about tax rates or land boundaries, a modern quarrel he could easily subvert with state bureaucracy and borrowed money. He was entirely unprepared for a theological reckoning, a trial by ancestry.

In the secluded, inner court of Nana Adwoa's compound, the elders and key women gathered once more. The atmosphere was somber, heavy not with fear, but with the weighty, complex responsibility of success. They had succeeded in firing their most potent weapon, but the victory was merely procedural; the immense labor of managing the fallout remained.

"The silence is a necessary stage, but it is dangerous," Nana Adwoa observed, her voice barely above a whisper, yet commanding the attention of Opanyin Manu and her daughter, Akua Safoa. "It breeds doubt among the fearful, and it gives him time to prepare his political lie. We must use this waiting period to address the two fundamental consequences of his rule. We must prepare not for a trial, but for the cleanup of a wreck."

The two consequences, discussed in low, measured tones, formed the thematic pillars of their immediate concern: Ancestral Retribution (the spiritual consequence) and Political and Financial Ruin (the modern consequence).

Opanyin Manu, the retired teacher whose precise hand had drafted the Statement, adjusted his spectacles and spoke with the measured authority of historical knowledge. "The most immediate and terrible consequence, Nana Adwoa, is not the money he has taken, but the moral injury he has inflicted upon Amansankrom. He has repeatedly violated the Akwasidae Covenant. He has desecrated the Grove. He has shown no respect for elders—living or dead. This invites Ancestral Retribution."

He paused, looking around the circle, his expression grim. In the Kwahu worldview, this retribution was not a simple flash of divine anger, but a slow, systemic unraveling of fate, a poisoning of the communal well.

"This is not superstition," he stated firmly. "It is the law of cause and effect in the moral realm. The Chief has broken the essential political contract that keeps our world ordered. The spiritual consequence is that the moral fiber of the community decays. It means the rains fail not because of the climate, but because the ancestors withhold the blessing. It means the children are sick not because of sanitation, but because the foundational purity of the town is compromised. Even if the Regional House of Chiefs destools him tomorrow, the Asumang—the spiritual pollution—he has left behind will remain. We must prepare for the ritual cleansing, for the necessary labor of spiritual healing, not merely for the political judgment."

Akua Safoa, whose own life had been marked by the immediate, practical sting of the Chief's tyranny, found herself in complete agreement. The anxiety she felt was no longer about the market tax or the timber debt; it was about the sickening feeling of living in a town whose spiritual protector was its greatest spiritual vandal.

"The rot goes deeper than the bank accounts, Opanyin," she affirmed. "I feel it in the market. The women trust each other less. The price gouging is worse. People are more willing to cheat their neighbors because the Chief has taught us that greed is the only law. We are fighting for our Kwahu origins—

the very definition of who we are as a principled, organized community."

Nana Adwoa nodded, bringing the discussion back to the equally catastrophic modern reality. "Precisely. We are fighting not for revenge, but for the right to heal. The second consequence is the Political and Financial Ruin. Kwaku Bonsam did not merely steal; he tied Amansankrom into a thousand knots of debt and corrupted contracts with outside entities. When he is removed, we will inherit a legacy of legal disaster."

She elaborated on the complexity of the modern ruin, a challenge that even righteous governance could take a decade to overcome. "He has leased communal lands for fifty years in exchange for personal commission. He has signed over the rights to our mahogany timber to foreign loggers under contracts that are legally binding in Accra, regardless of their immorality in this context. He has leveraged the Stool's limited funds as collateral for his own bad loans.

When the new Chief, the rightful and chosen custodian, takes the Stool, he or she will be confronted by a legal debt crisis that threatens to bankrupt the town entirely. The Asumang is spiritual debt; the timber contracts are financial debt. Both must be cleared, and clearing the latter will take every ounce of our communal discipline."

The conversation intensified, turning to the heavy weight of this inheritance. Opanyin Manu worried aloud about the inevitable chieftaincy litigation that would follow Kwaku Bonsam's removal—the opportunists and rival families who would exploit the chaos to press their own claims. This was the curse of modern corruption: it did not just wound the immediate victim; it destabilized the entire political infrastructure, creating endless opportunities for new, lesser tyrants to rise.

"The greatest challenge is not the Chief himself," Nana Adwoa concluded, resting her case with quiet authority, "but the normalization of corruption he has achieved. We must prove to the people that a return to honor, to respect for elders and the Sankofa principle of retrieving necessary morality, is the only sustainable economic path. If we fail, the Chief's ruinous legacy will continue long after he is gone, manifesting as endless court battles and financial servitude to the very foreign interests he invited."

The discussion of this dual catastrophe—spiritual blight and financial collapse—served its purpose: it sobered the elders, preparing them for a long, difficult process of restoration, ensuring their focus remained on the healing of the town rather than the momentary satisfaction of the Chief's destoolment.

The conference came to a close, and the quiet, deeply personal truth of one family's sacrifice took precedence over the great intellectual burden of the town's destiny. As Kobina drew near, Akua Safoa saw a change in his gait—a man now trudging over the rubble of his past.

The loss was concrete and irreversible. The timber contract, the economic engine of their future, had been officially terminated by the Chief's office days after Kobina affixed his signature to the Statement of Heritage. Kwaku Bonsam, still acting on the political information he understood—punishing a perceived financial defector—had successfully executed Kobina's greatest fear. The logging lorry, their greatest asset, was impounded at the local police station under dubious claims of licensing violations orchestrated by the Chief's men. Their accounts were frozen. The fear that had paralyzed Kobina for months had manifested, fulfilling its grim prophecy.

Akua led him to the far corner of the compound, where a small, carved wooden seat rested beneath a protective awning. They sat together, surrounded by the ordinary sounds of the evening—the distant cry of children, the clatter of cooking pots—a quiet, domestic counterpoint to the enormity of their loss.

Akua began, her voice soft but direct, avoiding the pity he neither wanted nor deserved. "It is done, my husband. The contract is lost. The lorry is gone for now. The ruin you feared has come."

Kobina did not flinch. He sat straight, his shoulders, usually bowed by worry, held in a position of quiet dignity. He looked directly at the oil lamp casting its warm glow, its light a symbol of the inner truth he had chosen.

"Yes, Akua. The ruin came. But it came after I signed the document. Not before."

He reached out and took her hand, a gesture of solidarity they had not shared since the market confrontation. This was not the broken, fearful man, but a redeemed man who had faced his shadow and found his way back to the Kwahu origins of his true identity.

"When the police came for the lorry, I felt the cold realization of the cost," Kobina confessed, his voice rough with emotion. "I felt the loss of the money, the loss of the years of labor spent building that trade. But then, an odd thing happened. The fear—the crushing weight of the fear that had kept me silent and kept me away from you—it simply lifted. It vanished like the morning mist when the true sun rises."

He turned to her, his eyes clear and resolute. "I had paid the price, Akua. I had paid the price for my courage, and the Chief had nothing left to hold over me. He took the lorry, but he could not take the honor I found in that one, small act of putting my name beneath Opanyin Manu's. He could not take the knowledge that I stood with Nana Adwoa and with the ancestors, not with his corrupt, decaying modernity."

This was the key moment of redemption. Kobina had measured his dignity in terms of the lorry's value and the timber contract's profit; he now understood that his dignity was priceless, rooted in the unwritten laws of his people. He had finally embraced the core principle of respect for elders in its truest form: respect for the elders who uphold the moral code, not merely for the man who wears the title.

Akua Safoa's heart swelled with a quiet, powerful pride that superseded the pain of financial loss. She had her husband back—a husband of moral courage, aligned entirely with her life's work. "You have bought back your soul, Kobina. The

Chief asked for your livelihood, but you gave him your truth. And your truth is far more powerful than his lorry."

Kobina leaned back against the wall, the tension easing out of his body. He spoke thoughtfully, connecting his personal struggle to the larger thematic discussion the elders had just concluded. "I had always feared the Political and Financial Ruin most keenly. I believed that money was the shield against chaos. But Kwaku Bonsam taught me that the opposite is true. His love of money was the chaos. His corruption was built on the foundation of greed, and that foundation can never hold a community."

He reflected on the spiritual dimension, his newfound perspective offering a profound, sobering insight into the town's future. "The loss of the timber contract is a wound, yes, but it is a clean wound, Akua. We know where the injury is. The spiritual pollution he has caused—the Ancestral Retribution—that is the unseen, chronic sickness that threatens our children. We chose to fight the pollution. The financial loss is simply the cost of the medicine."

The gravity of the situation was immense, yet the shared understanding between husband and wife was their newfound strength. They recognized that the loss of the lorry was merely the initial, personal manifestation of the wider economic collapse Nana Adwoa had predicted. They were now financially destitute, but morally whole.

"What do we do now, Kobina?" Akua asked, her gaze fixed on him, asking not for direction, but for confirmation of their shared path. "The rebuilding must begin at home."

Kobina smiled faintly, the smile of a man who has made peace with his fate. "We do what our ancestors did, Akua. We start small. We do what we can with our hands. We will go back to the cocoa farm. The Chief may have the contracts for the big timber, but he cannot steal the small farm where we grew up. We will nurture that small plot back to health. We will use the money we have saved for the children's fees, and we will find a way, knowing that we have dignity. We have given the town the weapon of documented truth; now, we must give the town the example of dignified financial survival against the odds."

This shared resolution was the essence of the better future they aspired to. It was a future stripped of the modern excesses the Chief had championed, built instead on the foundational virtues of the Kwahu origins—hard work, community trust, and an unshakeable belief in the moral order. The immediate consequence of Kwaku Bonsam's rule had been pain and loss, but that pain had acted as a powerful crucible, forging a deeper, more resilient strength in those who chose honor over wealth.

Their quiet reconciliation and unified resolve marked the true turning point in the community's resistance. Kobina Osei's signature, once a source of terror, was now a powerful symbol of redemption, encouraging others to realize that the cost of silence was infinitely higher than the cost of resistance. They had lost their livelihood, but they had secured their honor, and in the Kwahu tradition, honor was the only currency that guaranteed a true, enduring better future. The silence of the Registrar continued, but for Akua and Kobina, the internal turmoil had ceased. The wait was now external, focused entirely on the distant thunder of political consequences, and they were ready for the storm. Their redemption was complete, and the stage was set for the town's larger healing.

The town of Amansankrom fell into a strange quiet after the letter was sent out. Everyone was waiting for the Regional House of Chiefs to strike Kwaku Bonsam down. But Nana Adwoa warned them that simply waiting was not enough. The consequences of the Chief's bad rule were no longer something they just talked about; they were everywhere, plain to see. The town needed to know the real damage. They had to see the full list of things they had to fix.

Nana Adwoa sent a small group out on a tour. It was not a protest walk, but a solemn counting of the losses. Akua Safoa accompanied Opanyin Manu, the old teacher, and two young men, strong in body and quiet in spirit, who would serve as their lookouts. Their job was to document the wreckage, to link Kwaku Bonsam's greed directly to the visible decline of their home.

They needed to pause the legal fight for a moment, to truly assess the destruction, so that when rebuilding started, they would remember how deep the wounds ran.

Their first stop was the high ground, where the rolling hills should have been thick with the dark green leaves of healthy cocoa plants. These were the rich plots that the Chief had been seizing one by one, claiming he would use them for grand, new developments.

They stopped at Mama Serwah's plot. This was the small farm whose loss had caused that terrible, public wail from Mama herself, the cry that started the resistance. What they saw was heartbreaking.

"Look at this," Akua whispered, her voice tight with anger and sorrow. "Three seasons it has been like this."

The land was fallow. There were no strong shade trees, nor were there any carefully pruned cocoa plants. Only dry, tangled brush and weeds that thrived where honest crops died. Kwaku Bonsam had evicted Mama Serwah with a promise of a future hotel or a big logging deal. Yet, nothing had been built. The site was just a mess of dirt and dead wood.

Opanyin Manu stepped carefully through the tangled vines, his walking stick tapping the hard ground. "The promise was a lie, Akua. The project was never about production. It was only about taking."

He sighed deeply, adjusting his cloth on his shoulder. "This ground proves it. Corruption yields no harvest. You steal the farmer's work, and the land itself refuses to grow for the thief. It's a law of nature, and a law of our Kwahu ethics."

The failure was not just on this one farm. As they walked further, they saw the deep, unhealthy changes everywhere. The farmers used to work together, sharing labor and looking out for each other's plots. That communal farming was gone.

"They are terrified to help each other now," one of the young men, Kofi, said softly. "They fear his tax collectors will see them working hard and simply charge them more."

The atmosphere was thick with individualized fear and suspicion. Farmers were afraid to leave their tools, afraid to leave their fields, afraid even to talk about how much they were yielding. Kwaku Bonsam's paranoia had forced them into loneliness. The small farms were being worked by worried, isolated people, which made the whole town less efficient and poorer.

Akua shook her head. "He did not just take the money. He broke the solidarity that makes us Kwahu. He cut the cord of trust between neighbors."

The ruined fields showed the spiritual consequence plainly. They saw that the curse Nana Adwoa spoke of was not a sudden burst of lightning, but this slow, sickening failure of the earth when the spirit of the community was stolen.

Next, they traveled to the communal water source. This spring, deep in the hills, was more than just drinking water; it was the town's lifeblood. For hundreds of years, it had been a pure gift from the ancestors, a gathering place for women, guarded by sacred tradition. Its purity was the town's pride.

When they arrived, a heavy silence fell over the group. The air tasted wrong.

"Oh, my fathers," Opanyin Manu whispered, crossing his arms over his chest in a gesture of deep distress. "This is a crime."

A thick, ugly plume of rust-colored dirt and oily sludge was running straight into the spring's collection basin. It stained the usually clear water, turning it murky and undrinkable.

They followed the pollution uphill, quickly finding its source. It came from one of the Chief's own massive, private construction sites. It was supposed to be a grand palace or maybe a hotel for his friends, but the project had stalled, abandoned like the cocoa farms. The site was a jarring skeleton of concrete and rusting steel high on the mountainside.

The builders, obeying only the Chief's will, had ignored every traditional rule. They had stripped the land of its protective plants, making a raw scar on the earth. Every rainstorm washes the residue of cement and earth down the hill, channeling it perfectly into the spring.

"He has poisoned the shared lifeblood by self-interest," Akua said, her voice shaking with quiet fury. She felt the violation deeply. This was beyond money. This was an attack on the physical health and spiritual safety of the whole town.

Opanyin Manu pointed at the ugly, unfinished concrete palace looming above the spring. "That ruin is a monument to his selfishness. He cares more for the concrete slab for his own vanity than for the clean water that keeps our children alive. A true Chief protects the land and the water. Kwaku Bonsam has done the opposite."

Akua knelt down near the polluted stream, looking at her distorted reflection in the muddy surface. "How can we even begin to clean this up? It is not just pipes that are broken; it is the promise of purity. This pollution is the physical sign of the spiritual pollution he has brought upon Amansankrom. It demands more than just a new Chief; it demands a cleansing."

They stayed there for a long time, the stench of the polluted water a constant reminder of the depth of the betrayal. Reversing this environmental disaster would be expensive and slow, needing not just tools, but a complete change of heart and respect for the earth they lived on.

The final destination was the market square. This bustling place had always been the throbbing heart of the community and the foundation of the women's power base. It was usually loud, vibrant, and alive with trade.

Today, it was startlingly quiet. The market was half-empty.

Akua, the market woman, felt the emptiness in her bones. The rows of tables and stalls, which should have been overflowing with plantain, cloth, and smoked fish, now showed large, depressing gaps. This was the most painful evidence of the economic consequences of misrule.

"Where is Mama Fosuah?" Akua asked, pointing to a vacant stall. "And Auntie Mansa, who sells the soap?"

A small group of women still trading nearby looked up, their expressions weary. A woman named Ama, selling garden eggs, spoke up quietly. "They couldn't pay the new taxes, Akua. They tried to bargain, but the Chief's clerk just laughed and seized their remaining stock. They've gone back home to sell from their doorsteps, if they sell at all."

The women who remained were subdued. They traded quickly and kept their voices down. The laughter was gone. The long, easy conversations were gone. The Chief had managed to destroy the moral economy by ensuring that profit was instantly met with punishment. The great engine of Amansankrom was spluttering.

"He thought that by crushing the market, he could crush us," Akua said, looking around. "He thought he could silence the women's voices by starving their tills."

Opanyin Manu nodded slowly. "The market is trust, Akua. The health of the market shows the health of the community's trust. When the Chief destroys that trust, the trade dies. We must restore that faith, not just remove the taxes."

Despite the emptiness, Akua saw a small sign of hope. The remaining traders were gathered in small, tight knots. They weren't discussing prices; they were quietly sharing information about the legal case, the Chief's movements, and the families who needed help. Kwaku Bonsam's greed had tried to isolate them, but the shared struggle had only forged a deeper solidarity.

The True Challenge: Sankofa in Practice

When the group returned to Nana Adwoa's compound, they brought back not just reports, but the heavy reality of the land's suffering. They had seen the fallow farms, the poisoned spring, and the ghost of a market.

Nana Adwoa listened, her face grave, and then spoke, bringing the terrible pictures together into a clear path forward.

"We have fired the legal gun," she said, her voice carrying certainty. "The political solution is coming. But what you have seen today proves that merely removing the Chief is only the first breath. The real work is the spiritual and communal rebuilding."

She stressed that the sickness was not the Chief, but the decay he had left behind.

"The ruin is the ancestors telling us that we failed them," Nana Adwoa explained. "They did not strike with fire. They simply let our broken society fall apart. The water gets dirty, the farms stop giving, and the market closes. To reverse this, we must not just appoint a new leader. We must perform Sankofa in practice."

Sankofa, the principle of going back to retrieve what is valuable from the past, became their guiding light. They had to return to the honest, communal ways of their Kwahu origins that Kwaku Bonsam had abandoned.

The work they faced was huge, spanning three critical areas of communal life. First, they had to tackle Rebuilding Trust, which meant ending the fear and suspicion that had divided neighbors. They needed to show the entire town, every day, that solidarity was back, proving that working together was the only way forward and that greed would no longer rule their interactions.

Second, they had the urgent task of healing the Earth; the polluted water source and the scarred land needed immediate care, a duty they recognized as sacred and not just a matter of engineering. The new leadership had to commit fully to the earth's well-being over any pursuit of quick financial profit.

Finally, they had to focus on restoring the Moral Economy, which required the market to reopen, full and thriving. This demanded not only stopping the cruel taxes but also establishing a new, honest system that guaranteed fairness and transparency, thereby restoring the fundamental faith that hard work would be rewarded, not punished.

The insight they gained was final and undeniable: the solution was not only about law and politics. It was about the spirit of the people. They had secured the legal mechanism to remove the Chief; now, they had to prepare the town itself for the hard, necessary work of healing. The waiting was over. The planning for the true rebuilding of Amansankrom had begun.

The following afternoon, the community gathered again. This time, there was no need for the secrecy of the assembly room. This time, they met in the open, beating sunlight, under the vast, sheltering canopy of the ancient silk-cotton tree.

The location mattered. This magnificent tree stood just outside the edge of the Akwasidae Grove, the sacred space that Kwaku Bonsam had disgraced. By meeting here, visible to the whole town and out from under the shadow of the desecrated past, they signaled a commitment to transparency and renewal. The air, no longer heavy with conspiracy, vibrated instead with anticipation.

The people came—not just the market women and the aggrieved elders, but whole families. The men, their fear broken by the sight of Kobina's courage, stood shoulder to shoulder with their wives. The mood was serious but charged with a fragile, powerful energy. They had faced the weight of the ruin. Now, they were ready to weave the tapestry of hope.

Nana Adwoa and Opanyin Manu stood at the base of the great tree, their faces washed in the dappled light. Akua Safoa was beside them, her posture radiating the confidence of someone who had won the right to speak.

"We have seen the sickness," Nana Adwoa began, her voice clear and strong. "We have seen the poisoned water and the empty farms. But sickness is only half the story. Today, we must speak to the other half. What is the healing? What is the life we are fighting to build back?"

She invited them to speak. Slowly, the townspeople began to articulate their collective hopes and aspirations, each person adding a thread to the tapestry.

A farmer named Yaw, who had lost a patch of plantain to the Chief's men, was the first to speak with real passion. His voice trembled slightly, but it was not from fear.

"I want to farm again without checking the horizon every five minutes," Yaw said, gripping his hat tightly. "I want to know that the sun warms the crops for my children, not for the Chief's greedy stomach."

An older woman, Mama Fosua, whose stall Akua had noted as empty in the market, spoke next. "I want the ancestral law to have more power than the modern greed. Our grandmothers taught us that the earth belongs to the people, and the people belong to the earth. Kwaku Bonsam acted like the land belonged only to his wallet."

A young teacher, Kofi, stepped forward. "My hope is for justice that lasts. Not just justice for today, but for tomorrow. I want the children I teach to learn that when a leader steals, the community has the right, the sacred right, to stop him."

This was the core aspiration: the formal recognition of ancestral law over modern greed. They needed the legal system to affirm the ancient moral code. The people yearned for a return to the ethical framework that had sustained them for centuries, where leadership was service, not ownership.

"It is not enough to get rid of this Chief," Opanyin Manu added, confirming their thought. "We need a system that says: never again. The law must protect our past so we can have a future."

The conversation naturally shifted to the social fabric, which Kwaku Bonsam had torn apart with suspicion and fear.

A man named Kwame, a respected elder who had been quiet during the initial stages of the resistance, spoke about the recent events. "We men were weak," he confessed, looking toward Akua and Nana Adwoa. "Kwaku Bonsam used our fear of losing face to keep us silent. We let the women carry the weight for too long."

He paused, a flicker of deep emotion in his eyes. "We owe a debt to Kobina. He was just a boy, but he showed us that protecting the women is protecting the whole town. My hope is that the solidarity we find now is not temporary. I want men and women to work as one body again, to rebuild what was lost."

Akua Safoa smiled at Kwame. This open admission was a powerful sign of healing. Solidarity meant ending the division between men and women that the Chief had skillfully exploited.

"It must be equal work," Akua agreed. "When the market was broken, the whole town starved. When the farms are fallow, no one eats. Our power is one. My hope is to see the Role of Women in Amansankrom written into the town's laws, not just our custom."

The air felt lighter. The simple act of speaking these hopes out loud, under the open sky, transformed them from private worries into a collective blueprint. The problem was no longer Kwaku Bonsam; the solution was Amansankrom itself.

Nana Adwoa stepped forward, bringing the discussion from the realm of aspiration into the harsh reality of political structure.

"The Statement of Heritage is traveling to Accra," she announced. "We have used the tradition to force the law to look at our problem. But we cannot wait for the law to finish. We must create laws that prevent this from happening again. We must make the solutions permanent."

She gestured to Opanyin Manu, who unrolled a large sheet of paper, a draft of proposals. This was the blueprint for the better future.

"We have identified three main problems that allowed Kwaku Bonsam to rule unchecked," Opanyin Manu explained, his voice taking on the clear authority of a teacher addressing a class. "And we have three solutions, rooted in Sankofa, that will heal Amansankrom."

Opanyin Manu pointed to the first item on the paper. "Kwaku Bonsam stole the land because he could sell it as his own. He pretended to have total individual power over the ancestral earth. That ends now."

Nana Adwoa took over, her words firm and decisive. "We must establish an irreversible, documented, communal land trust. We will write into the town's highest governing agreement that no single Chief, no matter how powerful, can ever sell or mortgage communal land without a clear majority vote from a community council."

A roar of agreement swept through the crowd. This solution was profound. It removed the root temptation: the idea that the stool lands were a Chief's personal bank account. The land would be legally documented as belonging to the Stool—not the individual currently sitting on it—protecting it for all future generations. It was a formal, permanent barrier against individual greed, codifying the ancient respect for the earth.

"The trust must be filed with the Regional Registrar and the local Lands Commission," Nana Adwoa explained. "It won't just be a promise; it will be a legal document that even the government recognizes."

Akua Safoa stepped forward to address the issue that had caused her the most pain: the market taxes and the theft of the town's wealth.

"Kwaku Bonsam thrived in the dark. He collected market fees and dues in secret, and no one could ever question where the money went. He used the town's wealth to hire mercenaries against the townspeople," she said, her voice rising with resolve.

"Our solution is financial transparency. We will create a community council for market tax oversight. This council will be made up of market women, elders, and honest young men like Kofi."

The proposal was simple and powerful: the council would receive all market taxes, pay them directly into a designated Amansankrom Development Account, and publish the receipts and expenditure every quarter for the entire community to see.

"The money will be used for what it was meant for: fixing the roads, cleaning the spring, and paying school fees for the poorest children," Akua declared. "We will put light on every penny. The time for secret wealth is finished."

The women in the crowd cheered the loudest. This was their victory, the guarantee that their hard labor would benefit their children, not the Chief's cronies.

Finally, Opanyin Manu addressed the fundamental flaw in the power structure: the lack of a proper, institutional check on the Chief.

"The Queen Mother, Nana Adwoa, is the Kingmaker. She nominates the Chief. But once he is enthroned, her power to stop him has been limited to custom and moral persuasion.

Custom, we have learned, is not enough when greed takes hold," Opanyin Manu stated.

Nana Adwoa finished the point, speaking directly to the women. "We must codify the Queen Mother's authority to intervene and check the Chief's power. This means the Queen Mother must have the formalized authority to demand a full financial and judicial review of the Chief's decisions."

She explained that if the Chief refused, the Queen Mother could trigger a formal complaint of destoolment with the traditional council. This change would write the Role of Women in Amansankrom into the heart of governance, ensuring that the voice of the community's maternal line could never be silenced or ignored by the occupant of the stool.

"We are not just fixing this Chief's mistake," Nana Adwoa concluded. "We are making the system itself stronger. We are making sure that the one who chooses the king also has the permanent, legal right to challenge his actions."

The meeting had transformed from an emotional outpouring of fear into a structured, forward-looking political movement. The people of Amansankrom were not just waiting to be saved; they were drafting the laws of their own salvation.

As the sun began to sink behind the Kwahu Ridge, casting long, peaceful shadows over the assembled people, the meeting drew to a close. The community council was already forming, names were being proposed for the land trust, and the spirit of hope was palpable—a thick, warm cloak woven from justice and solidarity.

Suddenly, a commotion erupted at the edge of the silk-cotton tree's shade.

A young man, barely older than Kobina, burst into the clearing. His chest heaved, and sweat streamed down his face. He was the brother of Afia, the woman who had carried the Statement of Heritage to Accra. He had been riding his motorcycle hard for hours.

He staggered to Nana Adwoa, falling to his knees, utterly breathless and wide-eyed.

"Nana… Nana Adwoa," he gasped, clutching a heavy, sealed envelope. "From Accra. From the Regional Registrar. It just arrived!"

Every sound in the clearing died. The entire town, hundreds of people, froze as one, their collective gaze fixed on the single, official document. This was the moment of truth.

Nana Adwoa took the envelope, her hand steady, though the anticipation in the air was dizzying. She carefully broke the seal—a deep red stamp that bore the seal of the Regional House of Chiefs.

She held the document up to catch the last rays of the sun and began to read, her voice strong and unwavering, cutting through the silence.

"The Registrar writes: 'To the Paramount Chief of Amansankrom, Nana Kwaku Bonsam... Be informed that the Statement of Heritage and Grievances, submitted by the petitioners on this date, is hereby received and acknowledged. You are formally directed to prepare and submit a full, written defense, addressing all matters of ritual and financial misconduct, within twenty-eight days. Failure to comply will result in an immediate hearing before the Judicial Committee.'"

The sound that followed was not a cheer, but a collective, massive intake of breath. The legal process had begun. The women's daring strategy had worked. The Ancestral Law had pierced the armor of modern corruption.

Kwaku Bonsam was officially challenged. His rule was no longer just a source of local gossip and fear; it was now a matter of record before the highest traditional court in the region.

Epilogue

Kwaku Bonsam's time left a town marked by scars. He had taken a strong community and reduced it to its bare minimum.

The damage was easy to see: the sacred Akwasidae Grove was ruined, the stream was poisoned, the communal land was sold, and the town's funds were gone. The market square was weak because of fear and high taxes. But the worst damage was the broken trust and the realization that their sacred institution could be corrupted by one person's hunger for power.

The town learned a hard truth: a chief is a servant, and when the service stops, his authority must end.

With the Stool now vacant, the real work of renewal began, using the plan they created under the silk-cotton tree.

Nana Adwoa, acting as the Stool's guardian, took immediate action. The first move was to protect the future. Documents for the Communal Land Trust were filed, placing the ancestral land permanently in the hands of the people, safe from any individual chief's desire.

The Financial Transparency system was established, with Akua Safoa and the market women forming the powerful new council to ensure every penny was accounted for and reinvested. The Queen Mother's Role was clearly defined, turning her moral voice into lasting institutional power, guaranteeing a check on the throne for all time.

The future of Amansankrom was uncertain, but it was well-earned. It was not a return to the past, but a march toward a stronger tomorrow, built on the difficult lessons of the past.

Kobina, the young man whose courage inspired the town, became a symbol of unity, showing the new generation that true honor is found in defending truth.

The people now understood their duty: the health of their town depended not on the person on the Stool, but on the watchfulness and solidarity of the community itself.

Amansankrom was entering a time of healing, a time of Sankofa, where past failures were used to build a resilient foundation. It was a place where ancestral law had defeated modern greed, where the voice of the market woman was now part of the governance, and where the community proved its spirit was unbreakable.

As the search began for a new chief, the town waited, no longer afraid, but with a quiet, powerful hope. They knew the next leader would be bound by the strict rules of accountability and openness they had sacrificed so much to achieve.

www.ingramcontent.com/pod-product-compliance
Lightning Source LLC
Chambersburg PA
CBHW071421300726
48976CB00004B/1198